This is a work of fiction. Names, characters,
businesses, places, events and incidents are
either the products of the author's imagination
or used in a fictitious manner. Any resemblance
to actual persons, living or dead, or actual events
is purely coincidental.

# Chapter One

Thud!  Boom! Bang! Lily and Joan looked at each other, fear written on their faces. Lily glanced at Arthur who was rocking and repeating nursery rhymes to himself. His hands were up over his face as if trying to block out some horror.

"This is close today," remarked Lily.

"I know. It's not just Arthur this time but me as well who's scared. I'm almost wetting myself here," replied Joan.

"I know the feeling."

Joan and Lily were sitting in the air raid shelter with Arthur, Joan's husband. The bombs were dropping repeatedly one after the other with no let up in sight. These raids had been going on for a long time now.

Whoosh, bang! The ground began to shake as if an earthquake had suddenly struck.

"Do you think our houses will still be standing after this? It's too close for comfort out there."

Lily shrugged, she had no answer to Joan's question.

"Even if ours are ok think of the poor blighters who won't have a home to go to after this lot," said Joan, after more crashes and sounds of breaking glass could be heard.

Arthur suddenly let out an ear piercing scream after another bomb dropped too close.

Joan put her hand on him to try to reassure him but it was to no avail. He was too far gone. He had fought in the trenches of the Great War and had come home a broken man like so many others. He suffered from shell shock and never recovered. The war they were now going through had exacerbated this and he was increasingly retreating into his own world where he was back in the trenches. In many ways he had retreated into childhood, repeating nursery rhymes continually. Maybe this gave him a feeling of safety, no one knew. Joan was finding it difficult to get through to him now.

"I wonder how much longer this will go on for. If it continues I won't be able to get to work on time," said Lily, a nurse.

"Who knows," replied Joan with a sigh.

"I think we should bring something with us into the shelters in future so we aren't sitting here twiddling our thumbs. It might help take our minds off what is happening outside."

"Maybe, but what? I'm not a knitter like you," said Lily.

"At the very least we could bring a flask of tea with us so we can have a drink. I'm parched," said Joan.

"Good idea."

They had just been about to sit down to a cup of tea when the ear splitting wailing of the sirens went off. They had just had enough time to get to Joan's to collect Arthur and get to the shelter before the bombs had started dropping. There was nothing they could do for now but sit and wait it out. The German Luftwaffe had to go back soon and give them a bit of peace, but who knew how long for. The raids were becoming more frequent as the weeks and months went by. It wasn't just London that was suffering but other cities and towns throughout the country.

Eventually after what seemed like hours the All Clear sounded. Joan stretched herself and gave a sigh of relief. "At least it's over for now. It was close this time, I was sure I was going to be deafened by the sound."

"I know exactly what you mean," said Lily.

They stood up and helping Arthur warily left the Anderson shelter. The sky was alight, a mixture of grey smoke and bright orange from fires. At least it looked as if they had got away with it on this occasion.

"Just think of those poor folk who are stepping out of the shelters to find rubble in place of their house," said Joan.

"Not just that but those who have lost their lives because of a direct hit. Any way let's get inside and have that cuppa, I'm parched," said Lily, stretching herself and yawning. She, like everyone else were so tired from lack of sleep, disturbed by raids day and night. The frequency of the raids was increasing which didn't help.

........

Thud! The post dropped through the letterbox. Lily stood up and rushed to the door with a hopeful expression on her face. Joan watched her and felt for her friend. She knew what her friend was going through, she had gone through the same agonies with her Arthur during the Great War. Lily came back with a doleful expression on her face. "Nothing from Jack again, I hope he is all right, I do worry about him flying up there. But there is something from Bobby." For an instant her sad face brightened

"I'm sure Jack will be fine," said Joan reassuringly. "You know how busy the Germans are keeping them lately with all the air raids. He is probably too busy to write at the moment. Anyway they would have let you know if anything had happened. You know that."

Lily gave a weak smile and sighed. "I hope you're right," she said. A tear trickled down her cheek talking about Jack and his possible fate. Her hand shook as she picked up her cup and some of the tea slopped in the saucer.

"Hey don't spill your tea," said Joan, putting her hand on Lily's arm to steady it. "We can't afford to waste anything."

"I know," said Lily. "I'm so fed up of going to the shops and finding nothing and then wondering what to cook," she sighed. "At least I'm only cooking for myself and haven't got to think of how to feed anyone else. The dreadful coupons are next to useless."

"Tell me about it, we're all trying just to make do in these difficult times."

Joan looked at her friend and sighed inwardly. She had never seen a real smile on Lily's face in the years she had known her. A smile that never quite reached her eyes. She always had a serious look on her face and in her eyes. It worried Joan at times because Lily was never free to enjoy life. She kept her house nice and smart with oak furniture which was in fashion at the time. Sometimes they would have the gramophone or wireless on but Lily never seemed to enjoy the music or the plays they would listen to together. They would sit at the dining table with a cup of tea. Joan missed the curtains at the window, now that they had blackout curtains as were the regulations to hide light that the Germans would spot and know where to drop bombs. Not exactly attractive but they had no choice but to put up with them. The strong tape around the windows they hated with a passion but had no choice if they wanted to prevent them from shattering from the force of bombs dropping nearby. All the rules and regulations that had been brought in due to this war. Life was becoming very difficult for everyone with everything being so scarce and shops were frequently empty.

There was one thing that really stood out for Joan and that was the lack of photos of family in the room. There were no pictures at all of Lily's family which always made Joan so sad. Lily was all alone except for Jack and Bobby. She never spoke about her parents. It was only at the outbreak of war that Joan heard anything of Lily's childhood. It wasn't fair. She deserved better but what could anyone do, they had to do the best they could with the hand they were dealt. They had been friends ever since Lily and Jack moved in about six years ago but Lily refused to be drawn on the subject.

Lily always dressed smartly with the latest fashion. Today she was wearing a nice floral dress with bright red and yellow. Her hair was neatly done in the style she liked. It took her time in the mornings to use her finger and comb, curling her hair around her finger but it was worth it. At 26 she always took pride in her appearance although it was difficult to buy new clothes with rationing. She was going to have to learn how to make her own clothes, maybe she could use the old curtains to make some dresses for herself. The material wasn't too bad and who knew when she would be able to put proper curtains up at the window to replace the awful blackout curtains they were forced to use. Oh well, she mustn't complain, there were plenty worse off than she was.

Now, Lily picked up the envelope from Bobby and opened it. She smiled when she saw the coloured picture with stick people and an attempt at what she thought was a chicken. She showed it to Joan with a proud smile on her face.

"That's good," said Joan, smiling at the childish picture. "you must miss him."

"I do, every minute of every day, but at least I know he's safe with Megan and Hugh away from these dreadful air raids. I'm so glad I didn't let him come back when nothing happened at the beginning of this war." She took another sip of tea before continuing. "I wanted him but Jack didn't think it would be quiet forever, he felt it was the calm before the storm and he was proved right. I am so glad he persuaded me to leave Bobby where he was." Tears appeared in her eyes at the thought of Bobby being so far away from her. "I miss them both so much."

"It must be some consolation knowing Bobby is safe though," responded Joan, wanting to be of some comfort to her serious, sad friend.

"Yes I suppose so," replied Lily.

Bobby was Lily's five year old son and had been evacuated to Wales at the outbreak of war. He was billeted with Megan and Hugh in a small village. Megan and Hugh were childless and were glad to have Bobby to look after and treated him as if he was their own, totally spoiling him.

"We were very lucky to get Megan and Hugh for him to stay with. There have been so many horror stories floating around of evacuated children being treated badly. Bobby is so happy with them, but I do miss him so much," said Lily. A tear escaped and ran down her cheek. "Him and Jack. This blasted war. Why did Hitler have to try to take over the whole of Europe and cause such chaos? If it wasn't for him they would be with me now and safe. Jack would be going to the bank and I would be taking Bobby to school and picking him up afterwards. We would draw pictures and play games together. I've been robbed of his childhood it seems. It's not fair. Who knows how long this war will go on for."

"I know. It's not fair but there is nothing we can do but get on with it. Come on, let's have another cuppa," said Joan, wanting to change the subject, for her friend was looking very morose. "I've just got time before I have to get back to Arthur." Joan felt powerless to comfort her friend. What could she say? Thanks to Hitler the world was a mess and a dangerous place to be right now. "I'm sure you will hear from Jack soon, that will cheer you up."

Jack was Lily's husband. Before the war he had a good job working in a bank. They met at the hospital where Lily was a nurse. He had been visiting a friend on the ward where she was working. It had been love at first sight from his side although he knew that was a bit of a cliché. He had been attracted to her serious, sad face and with her brunette hair she had looked so beautiful. He never had eyes for anyone else. When they went out on a date he couldn't believe that she was interested in him, that they were together. He only learned about her life after he proposed and realised there would be no one in her family who would be attending the wedding. Her grandparents were by that time dead, killed in a car accident.

When war broke out he had joined the RAF and was flying Spitfires. From what he said in his letters, he really enjoyed flying. He loved the feeling of being just him and the plane in the sky, as if he was the only person in the world. The feeling of power it gave him was more than he could find the words for. He and the spitfire were at one, as if the plane was human, they just worked together to get the job done. When he went to get in the machine he always spoke to it saying, "Hello old thing, how are you today? I hope you're going to help me get the job done and shoot down those bombers. We don't want them dropping any of their bombs today on dear old England. Let's get to it and fight for the country. We must stop Hitler from taking over anywhere else."

Lily was always expecting bad news that he had been shot down and killed. The silence from Jack didn't help those thoughts. He usually tried to write every week but now it had been a month with nothing. She couldn't help but expect the worst. Somehow it seemed easier to expect the dreaded news than to remain hopeful, that way she couldn't be let down if the worst happened.

She knew how busy the Germans were keeping him and she knew how tired he was as he often complained of it in his letters. So many men were being shot down and killed or taken prisoner. Jack had lost friends.  It was a constant fear of Lily's that she couldn't get out of her head. What would she do if anything happened to her Jack? She didn't think she would be able to cope on her own with Bobby to look after. When would this dreadful war end. There was the constant fear of bombing raids over London. Every time she went to work at the hospital where she was a nurse she saw gaps filled with rubble where buildings had been destroyed by bombs. The frequent air raids were getting to her as well. She would work all day at the hospital and then the nights were spent in the Anderson shelter so she was suffering from lack of sleep. The planes and bombs were so loud and the air raid shelters were not exactly comfortable. How she hated those shelters in the garden. They were made of corrugated steel dug into the ground. On the top there was a thick layer of soil and turf which helped keep them secure. Inside they were always damp and grim.  Lily called them monstrosities, she hated them that much, but they served a useful purpose and kept them safe from the bombs.

Lily and Joan joined each other in the shelter instead of each being in their separate ones. They enjoyed the company. There was also Joan's husband Arthur. Joan found it useful when they joined up in the shelter because Lily could help her with Arthur. Arthur was a very nervous man in his mid forties. He had fought in the Great War and had never recovered from the shell shock. He had seen and heard too much, too many friends killed and all the noise of machine guns on the battlefields. Now he had a tendency to get very jumpy when the bombs dropped. He would also rock backwards and forwards, obviously very distressed.

.......

While Joan and Lily were having a good old chinwag, Jack and the other pilots were sitting in the mess drinking tea and chatting. Jack yawned, "I'm so tired," he commented to Reg who was sat with him, "we never get enough sleep these days, what with the Jerries bombing most nights. They have been keeping us so busy I haven't had a chance to write to Lily. Knowing her she must be out of her mind with worry."

Reg said, "She knows what things are like so she'll realise you're too busy to write. Anyway, she'll realise she'd have been notified if anything had happened to you. No news is good news after all."Jack shook his head, and said, "You know Lily, she will be out of her mind thinking the worst." He took the photo of Lily out of his pocket and looked at it with love. "I always take this up with me, to remind me of her, to try to keep me safe. It's my talisman, my good luck charm. If I've got that with me I'll be safe." He gave a small smile but there was a look of sadness in his eyes.

Reg took a photo out of his pocket and showed it to Jack, "I carry this photo of mum everywhere with me so I know I have to survive for her or she'll have my guts for garters." He gave a huge sigh, "This war, what's it doing to us? We're getting old before our time, and so many will never have the chance to get old. We shouldn't have such worries on our minds at our age, too much life and death.   Every time we go up we don't know if we will come back again."

"I know," said Jack. "I don't know how Lily will cope if anything happens to me. She hasn't had an easy life and losing me might be the last straw. She doesn't have anyone to turn to except her friend Joan who lives next door. Both her parents are dead and her mum wasn't much use when she was alive, she was pretty much brought up by her grandparents and a neighbour although she lived with her mum."

"You'll be ok, you'll come out the other side and will be together again. We just don't know how long this is going to go on for," said Reg positively. "Anyway how is your Bobby?" asked Reg, changing the subject.

Jack smiled, and said, "He's fine. At least I know he's safe with Megan and Hugh. They're really good to him and treat him as their own. I don't have any worries there. He's happy. I've got his latest picture in my locker." He sighed, "I miss them both so much. I would love to have time off to go and see Lily and maybe travel to Wales to see Bobby but there is no chance of that. I can't even get a forty-eight hour pass to see Lily, and I don't see that changing any time soon while we're being bombed left, right and centre. Anyway, we had better get to the dispersal hut ready. We are up next when the siren goes off." He stood up and stretched himself.

It was September 1940 and the Battle of Britain was raging fiercely with German planes bombing if they got past the Spitfires and the other fighter planes trying to prevent them getting near Britain. The air raid siren sounded. They both jumped up. "Here we go again," said Reg as they rushed to their planes.

Jack got into his plane and started the engine. "Here we go again, old girl, let's go and shoot some more planes down shall we," he said to the Spitfire as the engine made its whining roar as it started up and began its lift off into the air.

As they flew higher and higher he saw sightings of a Heinkel 111, "Come on let's get this one shall we."  He started firing at the German plane and let out a loud cheer as the tail burst into flames. "Another one bites the dust."

.........

Lily and Joan were sipping their cup of tea when the, by now familiar sound of the sirens went off. They put their cups down and sighed. "Here we go again," said Lily. They rushed over to Joan's to collect Arthur and get themselves to the shelter.

"Come on Arthur, we have to get out to the shelter. It's ok, the noise will stop in a minute. Let us take you. Hold our hands, everything will be all right," said Joan coaxing Arthur. He reluctantly got to his feet and they both took his hands to help him.

Once there they sat him down and watched him sadly as he sat rocking back and forth repeating:

*"Baa, Baa black sheep have you any wool*
*Yes sir, yes sir three bags full.*
*One for the master and one for the dame and one for the little boy who lives down the lane."*

The rocking intensified, becoming more and more agitated as they sat there listening to the whoosh of the bombs and bangs as explosions took place. The ground was literally shaking as they got closer. A very loud ack-ack-ack from the ack-ack guns could be heard alongside the bombs just adding to the noise which disturbed Arthur so much. They hoped the guns would shoot down the German bombers that could be heard overhead.

Joan and Lily looked at each other. "They're close this time, this is too much. We only

had that raid earlier, and this one is just as close,"
whispered Lily to Joan, hoping Arthur wouldn't
hear her above his insistent repetition of the
nursery rhyme and the nearby explosions of the
bombs.

"I just wonder how much more Arthur can
take," whispered Joan back. "He seems to get
worse all the time.  He relives all the noise of
gunfire and battle from the last lot. I'm sure the
sound of the ack ack guns make things worse for
him, not just the bombs dropping."

"We can't possibly imagine what he must be
going through," said Lily.

"Last night I found him curled up on the
floor in a tight ball. It was hard to persuade him
that everything was fine and it was time for bed.
He was back in the trenches and tried pulling me
down with him, saying they would see me and
shoot and kill me if I didn't get down. He even
asked if I wanted my head blown off. I couldn't
persuade him at all that it was all right, we were
at home and it was time to go to bed." Joan shook
her head sadly. She really didn't know what to do
for the best anymore. She continued, "We will
never understand exactly what they went
through. So many men came back irreparably
damaged by the sights and sounds of trench
warfare. "

Lily reached out and took her friends hand.
She didn't know what to say. What was there to
say? Nothing she said would bring back the

husband she had known and loved so much, he was gone for ever, leaving this empty shell of a man behind. They sat in silence for a while listening to the noise outside and to the repetitious nursery rhymes from the broken Arthur.

As they sat there the noise outside lessened and eventually stopped. Later the sound of the all clear went off and they stood up with a sigh of relief, it was over, at least for now. All that could be heard now were shouts from rescuers looking for survivors in what was left of houses. Lily and Joan left the shelter with Arthur between them. All they could see around was smoke from the burning buildings. The acrid smell got into their noses making them cough and wheeze as they tried to breathe, their bodies screaming for fresh air.

"Come into mine for a while. Help me settle Arthur down a bit." They took his arms, one each side of him and slowly lead him down the garden towards the house and back in his chair.

………..

Jack landed with a sigh of relief, saying, "Well we made it back old girl. Let's go and see who's around and find out how everyone else got on." He got out of the plane, giving it a pat as he moved away from the machine and walked towards the mess to find out how the other pilots had faired.

When he walked in they were whispering and he instantly knew something was wrong, no celebratory slaps on the backs this time. He looked around hoping to spot Reg to find out who had bought it. He couldn't see him anywhere and hoped he hadn't landed yet. At the back of his mind though, he knew he wouldn't see his friend again, he just refused to acknowledge it.

He approached the group and asked, "What's happening."

Fred, another pilot, responded, "You're back then, we thought we'd lost you, we lost sight of you up there for a while and when you hadn't landed…" he tailed off not wanting to finish the sentence.

"Where is Reg?" asked Jack, wanting to find out about his friend.

"He was shot and the plane went down in flames. I saw it happen. There is no way he could have survived that," said Fred abruptly. This was typical of Fred, who was not known for his tact, believing it was best just to get to the point.

Jack walked out, needing to get away from the others. Reg and Jack had been close friends even before the war. They had both worked in the bank together and when war had been declared they had joined up. Reg had been best man at his wedding to Lily. Jack couldn't believe he would never see him again, that there would be no more jokes, for Reg had been a bit of a joker. He walked back to his plane and said to it, "He's not coming back, my friend bought it today." There was silence as Jack tried to get his thoughts together. He always liked talking to the plane when he needed to let his feelings out. He liked the silence he got from it, no judgement. He never liked the others seeing him when he was upset for he was a sensitive man and didn't like the others coarse humour, especially at a time like this. He knew their humour and jokes was just their way of coping with the danger they faced daily and the loss of other pilots, but it wasn't for him.

It was his sensitivity that had attracted him to the serious, sad Lily. It had been love at first sight on his behalf. When he knew her story he had fallen in love even more. She had to be strong to have gone through all she had and to have survived to be a caring individual capable of so much love. She hadn't been destroyed by her childhood like so many others would have been. He wanted to give her a better life than the one she'd had thus far. Her childhood had been very difficult and traumatic and he wasn't sure she would ever really get over it. He wanted to protect her from further trauma but knew that wasn't possible with this damned war.


………

Lily and Joan sat at the table drinking a cup of tea and keeping an eye on Arthur who was still rocking agitatedly and repeating nursery rhymes to himself. It was as if by repeating childhood nursery rhymes that he could retreat back to a time that was safe, a time of no responsibility, a time of being sheltered by his parents away from the horrors of the world.

Lily was lost in thought. "Penny for them," said Joan. Lily gave a shake and looked at her with her sad eyes.

"I was just thinking that if anything happened to Jack I'd  become like mum and then what sort of life is Bobby going to have. I don't want him to have the life I had." She sighed and her eyes glistened with tears.

"It won't happen like that," said Joan putting a comforting hand on her friend's arm. "You're nothing like your mum, you're strong and I'm here for you. You'll get through it for Bobby, you have to."

"But you can't be sure of that, no one knows how they will react to grief until it happens," replied Lily looking off into the distance, miles away as she thought back to her childhood.

## Chapter 2

**1918**

There was a knock at the door and Flo rushed to answer it, thinking it was her neighbour. Rose often had a habit of popping around at different times of the day sometimes for no other reason than to say hello. She opened the door with a smile to greet her friend. The smile died on her face when she saw a youth standing there. He was holding a telegram. Telegrams were dreaded by everyone as they usually contained bad news, especially by those who had someone at the Front fighting. This time was no different. The youth greeted her, handing her the telegram with a suitably sombre look on his face. Her face went pale as she opened the buff envelope and read the words: "We regret to inform you that Frank has been killed in action." For a minute she was stunned. No, it couldn't be true, not her Frank, he couldn't be dead. He was still alive, he had to be, maybe wounded but alive. This couldn't be happening, it had to be a cruel joke that someone was playing on her. Frank couldn't leave her, they had a young daughter, Lily to look after and bring up. She shook her head, then her face turned ashen and with a scream she fell to the floor.

Lily hearing the shrill sound rushed to the door. Seeing her mum on the floor she fell beside her repeating "Mum, mum what is it." Lily was scared, she was only seven and didn't know what to do or how to help her mum. It was obvious even to the small child that something was very wrong. At that moment their neighbour Rose was passing, took in the scene, and rushed down the path to see what was happening and to help if she could.

"What is it?" she asked the telegram boy. She reached down and picked up the telegram from the ground where Flo had dropped it. She quickly read it and took immediate action. Turning to the boy she said, "Can you take a message to her parents please and show them this and say their daughter has collapsed, they need to come urgently. I can stay here with the child until they arrive."

"Well I suppose so, but I am not allowed really. But maybe on this occasion it won't hurt." If the truth be told he was glad of something to do. It had frightened him badly when Flo collapsed and the child appeared, for he was only fifteen himself. He had been grateful when Rose came along and took charge of the situation. She gave him the address and he ran off. He had been eager to get away from there. That had been the last telegram of the day and he couldn't wait to get back to his friends and his easy life. He had to win his marbles back from Charlie, his best friend, who had won three of his the day before.

Half an hour later Flo's parents arrived and took charge of the situation. They helped Flo get inside and took her up to bed, believing sleep would be the best thing at that time, so she would wake up in the morning with a better grip on things and would be able to think of her daughter who still needed looking after. Lily's grandmother packed a few things for Lily so they could take her back to their house for the night and the next day if necessary, just to give Flo some space with which to grieve for Frank, her much loved husband who would never come home and she would never see again. Killed in some horrific way that they would never know or comprehend. No one could understand exactly what they went through on the battlefields of war, they just knew of the many losses during the whole ordeal and there was no telling when it would end.

Lily was taken home by her beloved grandparents after being told her mum needed a break, she was tired and would be fine after a rest. Lily was considered too young to understand what had happened and she could barely remember her father anyway, having been away at war for so many years. After all she had only been three years old when the war started and he went away with so many others, optimistic of defeating the Huns, so sure the war would be over quickly. At that time no one had realised just how awful it would be or how long it would last. Frank had never spoken much of the awful conditions they were forced to endure in the trenches. He preferred to write in an upbeat manner, not only to protect Flo from the horrors but also to keep his mood optimistic.

Lily had fully accepted what her grandparents told her and enjoyed herself fully with them as they were apt to spoil her. She was their only grandchild and now it seemed unlikely there would be any more grandchildren.

"Lily, we're taking you back to mummy tomorrow," said her grandma a couple of days later. "She's had a good rest now, and it's time she had you with her again. You must be really good for her though, as she is feeling a bit sad.

"Ok," she responded cheerfully. She was too young to think about what she had been told and to wonder why her mummy was so sad.

The next day she was taken home. Flo had changed in the last few days, her face pale and devoid of all colour, her eyes, usually bright and shining with laughter were now dulled and the ready smile that used to be on her face had disappeared. She had a blank look as if she wasn't quite there, as in fact she wasn't. She had retreated into a world of her own. Every noise and she jumped, imagining it was Frank opening the front door coming back from work. The table was laid with a place for him for when he was to walk through the door.

Lily's grandparents looked at each other and shrugged. They thought it was just denial caused by grief that she would get over in time. After all, surely it would help having Lily back with her to look after. What they didn't realise was that Flo would never get over the loss of her husband, that this sight was to become a permanent fixture.

Rose popped around every day to see Flo and to try to help out a bit by taking a hot meal in so Flo wouldn't have to think about cooking. She was concerned as the days went past and nothing changed. Flo still sat in the same chair, looking at the door as if expecting Frank to walk in any minute. Lily was starting to look dirty, wearing the same clothes all the time. She was only seven and couldn't be expected to look after herself. There was no sign of Flo looking after her daughter, in fact Flo didn't seem to register her presence, it was as if Lily no longer existed. Rose did her best and started washing Lily's clothes and helping her have a bath.

Lily, prior to this, had been an outgoing, friendly child always laughing and joking about something, but that had gone now, lost as she took on a serious, sad look, the result of having to grow up so quickly at such a young age. She had by now been told her daddy had died but it didn't mean very much to her as she couldn't really remember him. Her friends at school couldn't understand the change in her and withdrew from her as she turned up dirty, wearing the same clothes all the time.

After this had been going on for a few months Rose got together with Olive and Maurice, Lily's grandparents, to discuss the situation. They sat around the table drinking tea.

"I'm doing my best to help, but I can't do everything," said Rose with a deep sigh. "She doesn't seem to be getting any better. I'm worried about the effect this is having on Lily, Flo doesn't seem to realise she is there any longer, she just sits looking at the door as if she expects Frank to walk in any minute." She took a sip of tea before continuing. "Lily is also suffering, she no longer has any friends at school and she is becoming older than her years. Flo isn't looking after her. Her needs are being neglected, it's as if Lily isn't there, which she isn't to Flo."

"I know, it is deeply concerning to us as well," said Maurice. "We have talked about it but we still think Lily is better off staying with Flo. Without Lily being there then Flo might just get worse. While Lily is around there is a possibility of her improving over time and coming back into her right mind. Also it's in Lily's best interests to be with her mother."

"I don't know what to do for the best," said Rose. "Flo was always such fun but that has gone now and I'm not sure we will ever see the old Flo again. Of course I'm happy to help out where I can."

"Hmm," said Maurice, deep in thought. After a moment he said, "Maybe if we back off a bit and leave Flo she may start to come around and start to take care of herself and Lily again." He paused to take a sip of tea before adding, "We are making it very easy for her at the moment by keeping an eye on things and maybe that isn't the right approach. All this mollycoddling is encouraging her in this behaviour."

Rose started to say something but Olive stepped in, "This seems harsh I know but we have to shake her out of this somehow, it's time she got on with life and made the best of what she has left. She isn't the only one suffering here. Many people have lost husbands, fathers and brothers but they aren't wallowing in self pity like this."

Rose could see the sense in this but remained doubtful that this would work. She did agree though, that something had to be done. They agreed to try this tactic to see if it made any difference. It was agreed that Maurice and Olive would attempt to get through to Flo.

That afternoon, before Lily got home from school they tried to have a conversation with their daughter.

"Flo, we love you very much and know how hard you are finding things at the moment. We've been happy to help, but it is time you started to do a bit more for yourself and you have Lily to think of as well." Maurice begun.

Flo looked at them with a vacant expression on her face. Olive and Maurice looked at each other, neither of them sure if Flo was listening or whether she even knew they were there. Their heart ached for the daughter who had once been so full of life, but was now only a shadow of her former self. Were they doing the right thing, they wondered, but they had to try for what was the alternative, they didn't even want to consider that yet, if ever.

Olive said, "We've left dinner for you tonight but you will have to dish up for you and Lily and wash up afterwards. Tomorrow you can get up and get Lily ready for school as Rose won't be coming in to see to things. Do you hear what we are saying dear?"

Flo turned to look at them but made no response. They had no idea if she had even heard them, she just stared into space, looking straight through them. They left shortly after and hoped they had made some impression on their daughter. They loved her very much and wanted to do what was best for her. They just hoped these shock tactics worked, and would bring her back into the land of the living, instead of her own little world into which she had retreated upon hearing of Frank's death.

That afternoon when Lily got home from school she found everything the same as always, only this time there was no Rose to help out. Lily sat there, hungry and frightened, not knowing what to do. Eventually she said, "Mummy I'm hungry,"

Nothing happened, Flo continued looking into space as if Lily wasn't there and hadn't spoken. It started to get dark outside and still nothing changed. Flo stayed motionless, exactly as she was all the time these days. It was a very sad situation and one that showed no sign of changing any time soon. When it got completely dark outside and still Lily had nothing to eat she took herself to bed, tired from the day at school and from having nothing to eat. As was becoming the norm she cried herself to sleep, frightened and alone.

Lily awoke the next morning to more of the same. Rose didn't turn up with breakfast and to help Lily get ready for school. Lily had no idea what to do and as usual her mum was no help. The hunger pangs were becoming more insistent and by now causing pain in Lily's tummy. Not knowing what to do she sat there, hoping Rose was just running late and would be around soon. Rose didn't turn up. Lily felt abandoned and began to cry. Flo took no notice of her daughter's plight, still staring into space, totally unaware of Lily's presence.

That afternoon Lily took it upon herself to walk to her grandparents. Surely they would help, and she was so hungry. It was across the other side of town and Lily was not completely sure of the way, but she had to try.

Lily walked and walked, it was dark when she finally reached there and knocked on the door. Olive opened it and seeing Lily gave a cry and pulled her inside, wrapping her arms around the cold and hungry girl. Lily, knowing she was safe burst into tears. Maurice hearing the noise came to see what was going on and stopped in his tracks when he saw his granddaughter crying her heart out. He raised his eyes at Olive and she shook her head. They drew Lily into the front room and sat her down, still in Olive's arms.

It was Olive who broke the silence, asking, "What is it Lily?"

Lily looked up and in a choked voice said, "Mummy didn't give me anything to eat last night and this morning she didn't give me anything or help me get ready for school. Auntie Rose didn't come in as usual and I didn't know what to do so I came here. My tummy hurts and I am so cold." And the tears started again.

Olive looked at Maurice, their plan had obviously failed and Lily had suffered as a result.

"First things first, let's get you something to eat," said Olive, untangling herself from Lily's arms and getting up to go to the kitchen. Once away from Lily she gave a deep sigh, what were they to do for the best? Quickly she spooned out some stew that had been left over from their dinner and took it through for Lily.

Lily quickly ate it proving how ravenous she was. "Thank you Grandma," she said, gratefully.

"Right then, let's get you to bed, a good sleep and you'll feel better in the morning," said Olive, knowing full well that wouldn't solve all their problems but wanting to reassure the frightened Lily. What Lily needed was to believe that the adults would take all her problems away. Although Lily was learning from a young age that life wasn't as simple as that. The person who was supposed to love her and look after her had become a shadow of her former self and had retreated into her own little world, from which nothing could bring her back.

Olive stayed with Lily until she fell asleep and then went downstairs to Maurice to discuss the situation. "We have to do something, we can't let Lily suffer like this, it isn't her fault."

"I don't know," said Maurice with a deep sigh. "She could come and live with us but I still don't think that is the answer for either of them. They need to be together."

"But they are not really together because Flo is not present is she," said Olive.

"The other thing is to have Flo put in an institution that is experienced to deal with this sort of problem."

"That's a bit extreme isn't it?" responded Olive. "Do we really want that, she'll be drugged up and worse off."

As they talked, they didn't realise Lily had woken up and gone downstairs, needing comfort, when she heard them talking. "What's an instit, instit something?" she asked.

They turned to look at her, "What are you doing awake?" asked Olive.

"I woke up and got worried about what's going to happen," replied Lily.

"You don't need to worry," said Maurice. "We will make sure you are ok."

"What is that word you were using?" she asked again.

"It's an institution, it's where people like mummy can go if they're not well, where they can be properly looked after," said Olive. "You don't need to worry, we are just looking at what could help you and your mummy. It's ok," continued Olive, going over to Lily and putting her arms around her for she had started to cry.

"I'm scared," cried Lily, getting the words out in gasps through the sobs.

Olive held her tighter, feeling helpless. She looked at Maurice who also felt the same. She shook her head, not knowing what to say or do for the best which is exactly how Maurice was feeling as well.

When the harsh sobbing started to subside Olive suggested going back to bed, "I'll stay with you until you fall asleep," she said.

When they were settling into bed themselves Olive turned, to Maurice, "This can't go on, Lily is behaving older than her years, she shouldn't be burdened with this at her age. She's lost her friends, she looks as if she's lost weight and that smile of hers seems to have gone for good. I can't remember when I last saw that smile and always ready with a joke, just like her mother." She sighed.

"We need to decide once and for all what we're going to do. We need to act in their best interests."

"I still think it's in their best interests to keep them together, it would be far worse if they were separated." Maurice insisted.

"If they stay together in that house we will have to continue as we have been doing, if Rose is still happy to help out. It didn't work trying to jolt Flo out of it by leaving her alone with Lily. Lily was the one to suffer, and that's not right, she's just a child," said Olive.

"I agree," said Maurice. "We'll keep her with us tomorrow and speak to Rose and sort this out long term. We have to face facts, Flo is probably never going to get any better."

"I know," sighed Olive.

The next day exactly as decided the previous night, they went to speak to Rose who was horrified at learning the outcome of their experiment.

"Of course I'll help," she said, her eyes shining with unshed tears. "She was always a good friend. I'd do anything to help them. I feel like I've lost my friend which is exactly what has happened." The tears slid unchecked down her cheeks, mourning the loss of someone she had become close to. Physically she may have been present but mentally she had left them for a place they couldn't visit or reach. Flo had gone to all intents and purposes. Her life was a living death.

The only way she could be reached was to give her the one thing she couldn't have, her beloved husband, Frank.

Things continued in the same way over the years, nothing changed. When Lily reached eighteen she left home to train as a nurse in London. She couldn't wait to leave and all the unhappiness that meant. Before she left she asked Olive and Maurice why they hadn't taken her to live with them instead of leaving her with her mum.

"We thought it was for the best," they said in unison. Olive continued, "We did what we thought was best for you both. We hoped having you around would help your mum snap out of it. We realise now we were wrong. If only we could turn the clock back we would do, and we would have you to live with us. We love you very much and are so very sorry for leaving you to bear the burden of what happened to your mum." Maurice nodded in agreement.

"We know it may not be much consolation now, it's too late to change things but we really are sorry," reiterated Maurice.

Lily left the valley and went to London to do her nursing, never going back to the place where she had lived all her childhood and been so unhappy, for she couldn't remember a time when things were different. She didn't even go back for her grandparents funeral when Rose notified her, she couldn't bear the thought of it.

## Chapter 3

## 1940

Lily was on duty at the hospital on the men's ward. She liked the atmosphere there, everyone was always so cheerful even though many were in pain. There was always a lot of banter between the men and the nurses and quite a bit of flirting.

Ted was in, having had a hernia but was soon to be discharged. He was in his fifties so not considered eligible for active service. Whenever he saw Lily coming he couldn't resist calling, "Nurse, nurse."

"What is it," she asked, approaching the bed.

"I wouldn't mind another wash," he said giving her a wink.

"Come on Ted," she said, "You know you had one this morning."

Lily touched his wrist to take his pulse.

"Don't let my Winnie see you like this, she'll never let me hear the end of it. She'll get ideas and knock me over the head again."

"Maybe you should take another look at the wound," Ted said trying again. He knew he was pushing his luck. He wanted to be alone with her with the curtains closed.

She laughed, and said, "Good try, but not this time. Anyway I'm not sure your Winnie would approve of you trying it on with me. Look what happened last night." Lily laughed as she remembered the incident, as did the rest of the ward.

Winnie, Ted's wife, was a short, round woman in her fifties with grey, silvery hair which shone like precious jewels. She had a permanent twinkle in her eye which told anyone of her incredible sense of humour and mischief. Ted, on the other hand was of average height and thin. He was balding quickly as well. She was known by the whole ward. When she visited you could guarantee a laugh and that was exactly what had happened the previous evening.

Ted had been told by the doctor that he would be discharged soon but he had insisted he needed to be kept in so he could have a break from Winnie. She had, on hearing this, taken umbrage and decided Ted wanted to stay so he could flirt with all the pretty nurses. She had taken her handbag and begun hitting him over the head with it. The whole ward, patients and nurses, had been in hysterics over this. They knew Winnie by now and used to the way they would have arguments which always ended with Ted being hit over the head with the handbag. These occurrences were a daily sight and proved very entertaining for all concerned. It was like a free pantomime. Even the nurses laughed now, although at first had asked Winnie to keep it for outside the hospital as it was disruptive.

Lily jolted herself back to the present when she heard Roger calling her from across the other side of the ward. "Ooh nurse, you can touch me anytime. You want one like me, he's too old for you. I'll take you out somewhere nice as soon as I get out of here."

"I'm not sure my husband would like me to go out with another man but a good try." Lily smiled wanly at this exchange, thinking about Jack and wondering if he was ok as she still hadn't heard anything.

Ted seeing the sadness in her eyes called over, "You all right nurse? What does your old man do then?"

"He is in the RAF," she replied.

Roger shut up on hearing this. He had great respect for all those involved in the armed services. He would have loved to have joined the air force himself but his eyesight wasn't up to standard.

"Do you hear from him often?" asked Ted.

"I used to, but I haven't heard for a couple of months now," responded Lily.

Ted looked at her and had a feeling that it wasn't just not hearing from her husband that gave her a serious, sad face and eyes. It went deeper than that and he felt for her. He had so much fun and laughter in his life, he felt for someone who so obviously didn't. He resolved to speak to Winnie about her. For some reason Lily had got under his skin and he wanted to get to know her better and bring a real smile and laughter to that serious, sad face, and he was sure Winnie would feel the same. Yes, he would speak to his Winnie and together they would bring change to her life. Next time his wife came to visit he would put his proposal to her.

For all their arguments and getting knocked over the head with the handbag, they were a close couple who loved each other dearly and loved a laugh and a joke especially if it was at the others expense. Their arguments and him being knocked over the head with the handbag was all in fun, they would always collapse into fits of laughter afterwards. He knew when the handbag attack was going to take place and he would duck to try and avoid it but it never worked, he would still get it over the head.

. . . . . . . . .

Winnie came into visit at the usual time, watched by the rest of the ward, wondering what was going to happen this time. New patients were all being warned by the others to watch the fun although they were never told what exactly would happen. Ted and Winnie knew they were a source of amusement to the rest of the ward and were only too happy to bring laughter in the midst of illness and suffering.

"Winnie, we have to talk," said Ted when she arrived.

"Is this where you tell me you've met another woman," she responded, with a look in her eyes which boded ill for her husband.

"Of course not my love, you're the light of my life, you know that," he said.

"When you speak like that I know you're up to something," she said.

"No, no it's nothing really."

"I don't think I believe you," she said, with a certain look in her eye.

"It's about that nurse, the one with the serious, sad look on her face and eyes."

"I told you. I knew it was someone else," she said fiercely. She lifted her handbag up and knocked him over the head. The ward applauded, enjoying the free show.  Ted rubbed his head giving an "Ow that hurt!" cry.

A nurse ran over, saying, "We don't allow violence towards our patients," she said with a concerned look on her face. "I'm afraid I'm going to have to ask you to leave."

The ward erupted into laughter, including Ted and Winnie. Another nurse also joined in.

"It's ok," called a patient. "This happens all the time, they don't mean anything by it. It's all a bit of fun with them. They deliberately wind each other up and then Winnie gets her handbag to use as her weapon. No one gets hurt. Ted just pretends to be hurt by it and Winnie just pretends to be annoyed with him."

"Sorry, we should have warned you," said the other nurse, "We all look forward to visiting time. We also got caught out the first time we saw it happen."

"Well I guess the jokes on me then," said the nurse good naturedly.

"We need to talk seriously," said Ted, with a serious expression on his face.

Winnie, seeing that Ted was being serious and not trying to wind her up said, "Blinking well get on with it then, what is it?"

"As I said just now, it's that nurse that always looks so sad. We were talking a bit today with Roger over there and it seems her husband is in the RAF and hasn't heard from him for ages. But I don't think that is the reason for her sadness. It has to be more than that. We are so happy together and always ready to laugh and joke around, but I get the impression she has never had that in her life. She smiles and laughs but it never reaches her eyes, they still look serious and sad. I want to change that. It must be possible. What made her like that? We can't leave her ignore it. It wouldn't be right."

"She's really got to you hasn't she," responded Winnie, completely serious now.

"Yes she has, although don't ask me why. Goodness knows there is plenty of suffering in this world. But she has really got into my head and I can't get her out."

As Ted said this, Lily walked down the ward. "Had the handbagging yet," she asked Ted, with a smile.

"Definitely," he replied, raising his eyebrows at Winnie. She gave a slight nod to say she understood and had seen. There had been no light in Lily's eyes and the smile never reached them.

When Lily passed by, Winnie said, "I see what you mean, we have to do something, but I don't know what, we don't know anything about her, she is a blinking nurse and you are just another patient who will soon be discharged and then she will be out of our lives."

Ted shook his head, "We can't leave it like that, we have to get to know her and make her part of our lives."

……..

Next time Lily was off duty Ted decided to speak to the ward sister about her. "That nurse, the one with the serious and sad face, what's her story?"

"It's none of your business," responded the sister brusquely.

"She always seems so sad and I'm sure she is lonely as well. She has got into my mind and I can't get her out of it. I don't know what it is about her but she has really got to me. I can't ignore her. My Winnie and me are so lucky we have had good lives and have a lot of laughter every day, we make sure of that. I want it to be the same for that nurse."

The sister sighed. Lily had got to her as well. She understood only too well what Ted meant, but couldn't see what anyone could do. The sadness in her eyes obviously went way back before they had even known her.

"I know what you mean, but don't see what we can do about it, the past is the past, no one can change what has happened and obviously what has gone on in her life has had a terrible effect on her. All I know is she is happy in her job as a nurse. She is happily married and came back to nursing when war broke out and her husband joined up. I know nothing about her private life, she keeps very much to herself and doesn't say much. Anyway, you are only a patient and I have no business discussing the private life of a nurse with you," she said, finishing the conversation abruptly and walking off.

"Did you get anywhere," Winnie asked, when she visited later that day.

"No not really. The sister didn't seem to know anything and wasn't willing to discuss her with a patient. She did, however, reveal that the nurse has got to her as well. I don't know what we can do. We can't say anything to her with the whole ward looking on." Ted said, feeling helpless that they had come to a dead end on the subject.

"I know, but we can't do anything immediately. We wait until you are discharged, and then you are no longer a patient. We can approach her then and offer our friendship to her. It isn't guaranteed, she may not want to know, but we can only try, and take it from there." Winnie said.

She hoped Lily would respond to their offer of friendship, but even then there was no guarantee they would ever break down the barriers and get into Lily's heart. Maybe she was too broken, she didn't know, although she suspected not. Deep inside Lily must be a caring person to be such a good nurse and she did smile and laugh even if it didn't reach her eyes so there was a sense of humour present.

"When you get out of here, we'll go and see the Matron and have a chat with her about that nurse. If we explain ourselves properly she might be prepared to help us," said Winnie, determined not to be put off by the ward sister. There had to be a way and she wouldn't let anything or anyone stand in it.

"I hope you're right." Ted was totally discouraged.

"We can't give up and I won't allow you to either, or else," she said, holding up her handbag ready to do the deed.

"No, no, I give in, not the handbag, we'll do it your way and see what happens."

"Good," said Winnie, lowering her handbag with a chuckle. Ted had given in easily this time, but she would get him.

......

It was another couple of days before Ted was discharged and he and Winnie could put their plan into action. It was the next day that they came back to the hospital to see the Matron. They felt some trepidation but decided not to let it show.

"Make sure you behave yourself while we're here, no handbagging and no blinking with every sentence," said Ted giving a warning look at his wife.

"I know, who do you think I am! I will be on my best behaviour, I'm not stupid," said Winnie, lifting her handbag and bringing it down on Ted.

Once in her room they took a seat, looking at each other, unsure what to say. Matron was an intimidating presence with her stiff, starched collar and cap with a dark blue uniform that told of her status. It wasn't just the uniform that made her intimidating it was the stern face as well that looked as if it never cracked a smile. Her eyes were ice blue, so cold that they added to her general appearance. Matron's presence just filled a room and commanded respect and instant obedience. Many members of staff and patients were just a bit frightened of her, knowing her to be a strict disciplinarian. More than one person thought she wasn't quite human and saw her as hard as nails with no care or compassion in her. She was aware of how she came across and that was just the way she liked it. She felt this was the right approach and it got the job done.

"Yes?" she queried abruptly, to Ted and Winnie.

They looked at each other, quavering inwardly, at this imposing figure looking at them sternly, making them feel they were wasting her time. If they wanted to help Lily they needed to speak out and Matron was the only way forward, but right now she seemed like an insurmountable barrier getting in their way.

Ted took a deep breath and began, "Whilst I was in hospital recently I regularly saw a nurse who looked so serious and sad. I talked it over with my wife Winnie and we decided it wasn't right that someone so young should look this way, even in these terrible times we live in there are times of fun and humour, time to laugh and joke. We've been blessed with a good, happy life that we just wanted to share some of that with the nurse." Ted stopped abruptly, not knowing how to continue, faced with the formidable face of Matron who hadn't shown any sign of change in her general demeanour.

Winnie took up where he left off. "We want to get to know her. We want to show her there is some fun in the world, not just sadness. For some reason she has got under our skin and we feel we have to do something to help her. It would be wrong to ignore her pain which is etched in her face and eyes. I know we laugh and joke a lot but we really do care."

Matron was moved by their words although refused to let it show in her outward appearance, wanting to appear the stern disciplinarian that demanded respect and instant obedience and just a little amount of fear. She knew the nurse they were talking about and understood their feelings as she, too, felt this way about the sad Lily. Not many people ever saw this side of Matron and would have been surprised had it been pointed out to them. Inside she cared deeply about the staff under her and if in need or distress she would be there for anyone. Lily had got to her as well. She well remembered the day Lily was brought to her attention when she had to break the news of her grandparents death. There was very little reaction in Lily which told Matron so much. Lily must have had a difficult time not to react to the death of family members. Lily paled but that was it, there was a stone wall put up that seemed impenetrable.

"What is it you want from me?" she asked Ted and Winnie.

"We'd like to know when she finishes her shift so we can meet her and chat with her," replied Ted.

"And what makes you think I would do that for you. You're nothing to do with her, you were just a patient and she is a nurse in this hospital, that's it, full stop."

"Please, help us," pleaded Winnie, "We mean well and only want the best for that nurse."

Matron had heard about this couple from hearing the gossip from the nurses and was quite sure they were just what Lily needed to heal her inwardly and change from the serious, sad person she currently was. Lily was a good nurse and deserved something good to happen in her life and she felt these two were just the people to bring that to her, although she wasn't going to let it show to these two.

She rifled through the papers on her desk, looking for the rota. "Ok, so if I help you, what can you guarantee, I don't want any nurse of mine to be hurt," she said, needing to be sure in her own mind that she was doing the right thing. This was something out of the ordinary although sometimes nurses and patients did become attached but it always ended when the patients were discharged. This was not something she would usually encourage. The patient would get on with their lives and the nurses would move on. Patients came and went and they soon forgot about those who had left the wards, healthy once again. This time was obviously different.

"We definitely don't want her to be hurt, we want to befriend her and bring a real smile to her face not just that small smile that doesn't reach her eyes," said Winnie earnestly, looking Matron in the eyes, refusing to be intimidated by her stare.

Matron was a good judge of character and saw the raw honesty behind this couple's words.

"I admit, when Ted first told me about her I thought he was just wanting to flirt with her, but I soon recognised he was serious about this nurse"

"You should know I have only eyes for you my love," said Ted.

"Flattery will get you nowhere old man," replied Winnie. "I know what you were like with the blinking nurses, you were flirting as much as the other men on the ward. Don't tell me you weren't, because I won't believe you," responded Winnie spiritedly.

Ted knew where this was leading and chose his words carefully, not wanting Matron to decide against them. "It was only a bit of fun, you're the only one for me, my love."

Winnie lifted her handbag and said, "So now you're finally admitting flirting then, I knew it." She lifted up her handbag, bringing it down firmly on her husband's head.

"No, no, not again, ouch!"

Matron saw the twinkle in Winnie's eyes and knew she was doing the right thing. The talk about these two was accurate for once and not just rumours. Lily was definitely going to be safe with these two on her case.

"We don't condone violence in this hospital," she said, half-heartedly, knowing there was no harm meant, but not wanting them to see this.

"Sorry, Matron," they said together, meekly.

"As long as we understand each other," said Matron, firmly.

"Right," she continued. "The nurse you are talking about is called Lily and she isn't on duty today but will be working tomorrow morning. She finishes work at five o'clock," she said, hoping she was doing the right thing, but her heart told her she was. With these two around there would never be a dull moment.

Ted and Winnie thanked her wholeheartedly and left the hospital. "Whew, she is a right battle axe," said Winnie. "I'm surprised we got out of there alive."

"I know how you feel," said Ted, "I feel sorry for those poor nurses, having to answer to her. But do you know something, I think her heart's in the right place. I think there is a soft side to her."

"Yeah, I know what you mean, I'm sure she softened slightly as we spoke of Lily. And there was something in her eyes when I handbagged you. I don't know what you would call it, not a sparkle but something there," said Winnie.

"What made you do that, you daft apporth? You could have had us thrown out without another word. But I know what you mean there was something there."

"I couldn't help myself. Anyway I think that's what swung it for us," said Winnie with a grin, putting her arm through his as they walked off together.

Matron, stood in her office, looking out of the window, watching Ted and Winnie as they left. As she watched she was sure she had done the right thing. They would be good for Lily she was certain of that. That pair would definitely bring some fun into her life that was for sure. She might not have been so happy though if she had heard their conversation and realised they had seen through her stern exterior.

...........

The next day, Lily left hospital after her shift, tired as it had been a long day. She had been kept busy with new admissions and a sudden death of a post-operative patient who had been doing well. She was looking forward to getting home and putting her feet up. She just hoped they weren't going to be visited tonight, she didn't relish another night in the shelter, she wanted to sleep in her own comfortable bed for once.

Outside she met Ted and Winnie and was surprised. "Hello Ted," she said, "Are you all right, nothing wrong I hope?"

"No, no, I'm fine, thanks to all of you here," Ted replied, he continued, "We were waiting to see you."

"Me?" she asked surprised.

"Yes, we were wondering if you wanted to come to us for a nice cuppa. We thought we could get to know each other better," said Winnie. "I promise you, Ted won't be doing any blinking flirting this time, he wouldn't dare with me around," continued Winnie with a twinkle in her eyes.

"No, he wouldn't," agreed Lily with a smile, remembering the battles on the ward between these two jokers. She envied these two, with the closeness they so obviously shared, the love that emanated from their very bodies. If she were to admit it, they were a couple she would like to get to know better. She felt they would be good friends to have, a couple that would share good times and bad but still capable of much love and laughter.

"I can't today, I'm absolutely whacked out, and just want to get home and collapse into a chair. But I would love to another time."

"How about tomorrow or the day after then," said Ted, not wanting to leave it there, sure that nothing would happen if they didn't make a firm arrangement.

"I tell you what, why don't we meet on Saturday, I'm off at the weekend so won't be so tired." Lily said, not wanting to see the disappointment that had entered their eyes.

"Great," said Winnie with a grin.

They gave Lily their address and said their goodbyes.

Ted and Winnie watched Lily walk off, sure they could see a spring in her step, but knowing it would take more than that to take the serious, sad look off her face.

# Chapter 4

Saturday came and Lily got ready to go to Ted and Winnie's. She was surprised at herself for looking forward to it, even though it seemed a bit strange to be asked for a cup of tea at the home of an ex patient. The two had made such an impression on the ward that they weren't forgotten. Even now the nurses commented on how quiet it was without their presence.

She caught the bus and made her slow journey to Ted and Winnie's. She was saddened to see all the destruction that had been caused by Hitler's bombs and cursed him under her breath. There was rubble everywhere and ARP wardens still trying to see if anyone was buried underneath following last night's raid. There were people crying in the streets and wringing their hands hysterically while WVS volunteers tried to comfort them and gave out cups of tea. It upset Lily to see such misery and devastation everywhere she turned. When would it all end? It was some comfort to see how everyone was helping each other during this awful time. The British spirit hadn't been completely broken, everyone was united in the one common cause – to rid the world of the Nazis once and for all. They would win, Lily was sure of it, but how long would it take? How much damage would be done before it could be achieved? How many people would have to die?

Lily arrived at Ted and Winnie's house. A two up, two down with the front door opening directly on to the street. The street looked tidy and everyone obviously took pride in their homes, though tiny and clearly not well off. So far this area was untouched by the bombs. She had passed a public shelter at the end of the street that would, she supposed, be used by everyone, not having any garden for the Anderson shelters she and Joan had.

Ted let her in with a welcoming smile. He led her down a narrow hall through a door leading to the front room which housed a table and chairs. It was only a small room but was very welcoming and had a homely feel to it. Winnie was sitting in one chair but stood up when Lily walked in. She rushed towards her and enveloped her in a huge hug and held her against her large body. Lily, not used to such shows of affection, felt uncomfortable but stayed in her arms. Winnie let her go and looked her up and down. It saddened Winnie to see the serious, sad face of Lily who could look pretty if she were to smile. She had lovely eyes which would change her whole look if a genuine smile were to light them up. Winnie motioned Lily to take a chair while she poured the tea out which was already waiting in the teapot ready for Lily's arrival. There was also a slice of cake as well. Lily could tell they had gone to a lot of trouble for her and felt special. No one had made that effort before and it surprised and pleased her. She thought she had made the right decision to agree to come to them. She felt she wanted to get to know them as much as they wanted to get to know her.

"Was it a good journey?" asked Ted, as they sat drinking their tea and munching on the very nice cake Winnie had made that morning in spite of rationing.

"Yes, as good as it can be under such conditions, very slow and lots of rubble and debris everywhere." Lily replied. "I just don't know when it's all going to end."

"It's terrible isn't it," said Winnie. "So far we've been lucky, there's no damage around here. Every time we come out of the blinking shelter we dread what we might find. But still we have to make the best of it. It's not about houses which are only bricks after all. It's what's inside that matters. Memories are inside our hearts and minds not in our blinking homes."

Lily was surprised at something so profound coming from Winnie. For some reason she had thought these two people were superficial, all about laughing and joking. Winnie guessed at what she was thinking and said, "You seem surprised, we don't just have fun you know. Life can be very difficult at times but we still try to find the funny side of things even when we're hurting."

"Life can't always be a bunch of roses you know. There have been times when we have lived hand to mouth, not knowing where the next meal would come from but we just have to get by and humour is a good way of doing that. Life can't beat us," Ted said. He and Winnie wanted their new friend to know that they understood hard times, that life wasn't always easy but they had managed to get through because they had each other and liked a laugh.

This gave Lily food for thought. She had never seen things like this before, but still she couldn't get the thought out of her mind that if they had been through what she had been through they wouldn't laugh so easily.

There was silence in the room for a while as each was lost in their own thoughts. Lily was surprised there was such depth to this couple and yet they were still ready for a laugh and a joke. Ted and Winnie looked at each other, hoping they were getting through to Lily. They longed to know what had happened in her life to make her so serious and sad, but they had agreed they would not push her, it had to come from her.

"More tea," asked Winnie, taking the tea cosy off the teapot.

"Yes please," responded Lily.

"You are a good cook," said Lily, "That cake was delicious."

"Thanks," said Winnie. "I don't often bake because it's just the two of us and of course with rationing it's difficult but I wanted something nice for you."

At that moment the familiar wailing of the air raid siren sounded. "Come on," said Winnie "we have to rush to the shelter on the corner."

This was going to be a new experience for Lily who had never been in a public shelter before. Lily followed Ted and Winnie out of the house. She stayed close to her new friends as neighbours hurried out as well. The shelter was noisy with everyone talking at once. Some of the women got their knitting out. Winnie introduced the neighbours to Lily who smiled politely at them. She sat quietly not saying anything, just listening to the chatter around her and wondering how Joan was managing with Arthur.

"Earth to Lily," said Ted.

"Sorry," said Lily, "I was just thinking of my neighbour whose husband was badly affected in the Great War and now hates the sound of bombs and the ack ack guns. He thinks he is back in the trenches."

"That's sad," said Ted.

"I hope Joan got him into the shelter ok," said Lily.

At that moment someone suggested a sing song and then begun a rendition of Maybe It's Because I'm a Londoner. They kept themselves entertained going from one song to the next. Lily joined in along with the rest of them. She was thoroughly enjoying herself which pleased Ted and Winnie who kept an eye on her. Lily was almost sorry when the all clear went off and they left the shelter. There was such a sense of camaraderie there. She begun to see how Ted and Winnie had got through difficult times, although not well off they and the neighbours all helped each other. They didn't let life get them down, even now in the midst of this terrible war they were amusing themselves instead of worrying about what was outside. They left the shelter and although the smoke of burning buildings could be seen there was no damage close by.

Once back in the house Winnie said to Ted, "Put the kettle on love, we need another cup of tea, and this will be cold now."

"Me!" exclaimed Ted, "That's womens work. Us men put bread on the table we don't cook or do housework."

"Oh don't you," retorted Winnie, a dangerous look on her face.

"Of course not, I don't want to give Lily the wrong impression here."

"Hey, don't involve me," said Lily, a smile on her face, these two really were hilarious.

Ted and Winnie looked at each other and winked without Lily seeing. This was just what they wanted from their banter. Winnie lifted her handbag and whacked Ted over the head. The three of them burst out laughing. Winnie gave a small nod to Ted and he glanced at Lily who was having a good belly laugh as they called it. Her face was alight with laughter, she just couldn't help herself. These two were good for her although she hadn't realised it yet.

Ted got up to make the tea and went to the kitchen still chuckling to himself. He was under no illusions, it would take more than this to wipe the serious, sad look off Lily's face, but this was definitely a good start.

He came back with the tea and saw Lily wiping her eyes from the tears that had run down her cheeks. Winnie shrugged, it hadn't been that funny, but once started Lily hadn't been able to stop. She couldn't remember the last time she laughed like this. There had never been a reason to when she was growing up.

"You two are a right pair," she said breathlessly. She had laughed so hard she had become out of breath.

They were pleased to see this in Lily, it gave them hope that one day they would wipe the serious, sad look from her face once and for all. They hoped to find out what had happened in her life and longed to gain her trust so that she would tell them.

"Have you got any children?" asked Winnie, deciding it was time to get to know Lily better.

"Yes, a boy called Bobby, he's five. He was evacuated with the rest of his school at the outbreak of war. I really miss him and my husband Jack, he's in the air force. I haven't heard from him for ages."

Winnie leaned across and put her hand on Lily's. "I'm sure he's fine. You know how busy they are being kept at the moment with all the air raids. You'd have heard if anything had happened to him."

"Thanks, I know, but sometimes I just think the worst. Anyway, how about you? Have you any children?" asked Lily, changing the subject. This talk about her and her family made her uncomfortable, it was getting just a bit too close.

"No, we weren't blessed with children," said Winnie, a sad look passing across her face. "We always wanted children but it wasn't to be."

"I'm sorry, any child of yours would have been lucky to have parents like you," said Lily, wistfully.

Ted and Winnie looked at each other, they had caught the longing in Lily's voice. Were they getting to the crux of the matter. Her parents were obviously the problem then.

Not wanting to push it, Winnie changed the subject, "Do you like this tea cosy? I knitted it myself."

"Yes, it's lovely, you're obviously a good knitter. Whenever I try I end up with loads of holes." Lily laughed at herself. "Nothing comes out as it should."

"I could teach you, maybe that would help," replied Winnie.

"Hmm, maybe, but I'm not convinced," said Lily.

"Well, we'll give it a try. Knitting is a useful skill to have, especially if you have children." Winnie continued, "Do you hear from your son or the people he's billeted with?"

"Yes," said Lily giving a small smile. "I get a picture from Bobby and a letter from Megan and Hugh once a fortnight. They're very good at keeping in touch. Bobby's very happy with them. They treat him as one of their own. I'm so glad he's happy, you hear of so many horror stories of children being ill-treated by the people who have taken them in."

Lily glanced at the clock on the mantelpiece and sighed, "Well I suppose I should leave if I'm to get home before it gets dark. I've really enjoyed the afternoon, you must come to me next time."

"We would love to," said Ted, "when are you next off."

"I'm working next weekend but I have the Monday off, so we could make it then," replied Lily standing up.

"That sounds fine poppet," said Winnie giving Lily a hug. Lily flushed at the term of endearment. No one had ever used those words to Lily before and she felt uncomfortable.

"That went well," said Ted to Winnie, when Lily had left.

"Yes, I'm so pleased. I think we'll become good friends, she's a lovely girl."

"Her problem is obviously with her family, probably with her parents," said Ted. "I hope one day she'll trust us enough to tell us what happened."

"We must tread carefully though, we don't want to scare her off," said Winnie.

"It wouldn't take much I don't think," said Ted.

. . . . . . . . .

When Lily got home she popped in on Joan.

"You look happy, you've obviously had a good afternoon," commented Joan, pleased to see her friend look content for a change.

"They are so funny, and are very good company," said Lily. "Winnie is lethal with that handbag. Ted got knocked over the head again. When the siren sounded we went to the public shelter at the end of the street and had a good time. We all had a sing song together which passed the time and drowned out the worst of the noise. Everyone was so friendly and cheerful despite the situation."

"Sounds fun, I wonder if that would be helpful to Arthur, not that it matters really since we have the Anderson shelters," said Joan wistfully.

"They are coming to me when I am next off, I really want to spend more time with them and get to know them better," said Lily.

"That sounds good," said Joan, pleased for her friend. Up until now Lily didn't have any other friends apart from Joan, choosing to be by herself, probably scared of getting hurt and rejected. Her childhood had definitely left its mark.

"Arthur doesn't look too good," observed Lily. Arthur was sat in the chair, rocking and muttering to himself. "He looks paler than usual," said Lily.

"I know, I couldn't even get him out to the shelter today. It made him worse though, being inside with all the bangs," said Joan, looking concerned.

"I don't know what we can do," said Lily, helplessly. "We can't make the bombing raids stop. This war has a lot to answer for."

"All wars have a lot to answer for," said Joan, "it's always the innocent who suffer." She thought of all Lily had suffered as a result of war, not just Lily but her poor mother as well.

"I don't know how Ted and Winnie cope, they've obviously had difficulties in their life but they remain so upbeat and still manage to laugh and joke. They don't have money and a great sadness for them is that they never had children, but still they manage to make the most of life. Why couldn't my mum have been like that, instead of falling to pieces the way she did?" Lily said, longing for a different life than the one she had.

Joan put her arm around Lily to comfort her and said, "Some people are stronger than others. Your mum obviously couldn't cope without her beloved husband. No one knows how they'll react to suffering until it happens. Look at Arthur, he still suffers from what he went through, and will never get over it. We just have to get on with the hand fate deals us and make the best of it."

"I know you're right," sighed Lily. "I can't change what happened in the past and I can't change what the future will bring but I can choose how to deal with it."

"You'll be fine, I know you will," said Joan, pleased to hear Lily sound so positive for a change. She thought this Ted and Winnie would be good for Lily, and whatever happened in the future Lily would get through because she and they would be there for her. She really hoped the worst didn't happen and Jack came through alive and well but these days were so uncertain no one knew what would happen next.

"We had a letter from our Polly today, she hopes to get a pass soon as it's ages since she last had time off." Polly was Joan and Arthur's daughter. She was in her early twenties and was now serving in the WRENS. She was based in Portsmouth. From the letters she sent home she loved the work she did although she didn't speak much about it.

"That'll be nice for you both, I know how much you miss her," said Lily, pleased for her friend. "I just wish I could hear from my Jack."

"You will," said Joan.

"I keep writing to him and keep hoping there will be a letter from him, but so far nothing. Anyway I better get home, let's hope we have an uninterrupted night for once,"

"You're hopeful aren't you? I can't remember the last time we had a quiet night."

"I know. I'll probably see you later then." Lily went next door to her own house. Once she was sat down she sighed. She had such a good time this afternoon, she looked forward to seeing her new friends again.

.........

A couple of days later, just before Lily had to get ready to go to work the post arrived and when she rushed to the door and picked up a letter her face split into a grin. She hurried next door and when Joan answered she waved the letter in the air and said, "I've had a letter from my Jack,"

"That's wonderful news. How is he?" asked Joan.

"Oh er, I haven't opened it yet," said Lily, feeling stupid. She had been in such a rush to tell her friend that she hadn't looked at it.

Joan laughed and said, "You daft 'apporth why don't you open it and see what he says."

Lily unsealed the envelope and quickly read the letter. "He's fine, he's sorry he hasn't written sooner but they have been kept really busy with all the air raids." She paused as she continued to read. "Oh no, Reg was killed. They were good friends, Reg was his best man at our wedding. He got shot down and his plane went down in flames, there was no way he could have survived that."

"I'm sorry," said Joan, putting her arm around Lily's shoulder. "At least you have heard from Jack and you know he is fine. You can relax now."

"I know, but I still worry about him, who knows what may happen tomorrow. What happened to Reg could still happen to him."

Joan sighed, her friend could still be guaranteed to think negatively.

"Anyway, I best get a move on or I'll be late for work." Giving a wave she rushed off.

# Chapter 5

Lily was rushing along a corridor at work. The hospital was a maze if it was unknown, it took new members of staff a long time to get to know their way around and were forever having to ask, only to find they were going in the wrong direction. Lily, though, after all this time knew her way around with no problem having trained in the hospital and then working there. She left when she got married and when war broke out managed to persuade them to take her back as she wanted to do her bit to help and nursing seemed the best way.  As she hurried along in the direction she was going she overheard a strange conversation.

"Colin we have to do something now," said Eric. He and Colin were porters at the hospital. Eric had been there for a few years but Colin was new, he'd only been there a few months.

"Why the urgency all of a sudden?" asked Colin.

"My bosses are starting to push for things to happen soon or they are going to replace me with someone else. Things have to step up quickly. You know what things are like out there, I have to make a report on what we have achieved," responded Eric.

"We can't rush things or people will become suspicious," said Colin.

Lily stopped in her tracks and hid around the corner so they wouldn't see her there. What were they up to? She wondered. It couldn't be much really and she would rather not know. It was probably some black market racket that so many were involved in these days. With the food rationing there were lots of petty villains willing to take advantage of people's desperation for food and other things that were rationed. No one took any notice, there was so much of it going on, and she would rather not know what these two were up to, it was safer that way. Thinking they were finished she decided to step out and continue on her way.

"We have no choice," said Eric, "I am being put under pressure to get the job done. You are under me, so you do what I tell you, or it won't go well for you. If you choose to be difficult I will have to let the higher powers know and they will tell me what to do." Eric always spoke in very precise English.

"There's no need to threaten me," said Colin, "I'll follow your orders. I just wanted to remind you that people will get suspicious if things get rushed."

Lily heard this last bit and retreated to where she had been hiding, these were definitely not nice people and she didn't want to get caught eavesdropping. What she didn't know was that

Colin had seen her when she had attempted to continue on her way. He didn't want anyone getting caught up in this and decided he would have to warn her to stay away and keep her mouth shut. Colin was the nicer of the two porters and Lily was surprised at him getting caught up in something that was obviously illegal, as the black market was. She could only imagine that he had been coerced into it by Eric, who had always been a bit creepy as far as Lily and others were concerned. He was not nice to the patients either, being a bit of a bully, just the sort of person that would be involved in the black market. What she didn't like was that it was being run from the hospital, and Eric seemed to be quite high up in the criminal hierarchy since he reported directly to the boss. She wondered who the boss was, but it was best not to know and anyway was unlikely to be anyone in the hospital or they would have been involved in that little conversation. Not wanting to hear any more she retreated and decided to take a different route to get back to the ward. She put this incident to the back of her mind but didn't forget it.

The rest of the shift passed without incident and Lily went home tired as usual. She decided not to tell anyone what she had overheard, not even Joan. Instead she began thinking about Ted and Winnie and their forthcoming visit to her the next week.

A few days later when Lily was on her way to work on the bus she saw Colin get on and come and sit with her.

"Hello Lily, another shift about to begin, let's hope for a quiet one," he said, wanting to be friendly.

"Yes," said Lily.

"I wonder what damage was done in last night's air raid," he said, trying to find something to say to make conversation, he didn't want to come straight out with a warning. He had found out what bus she caught and had waited for her, wanting to find a reason to approach her without arousing suspicion.

"I dunno," responded Lily abruptly, she had no desire to get into conversation with this man who was so obviously involved in the black market and that meant he was nothing more than a common criminal in her eyes.

"Look," said Colin, coming straight to the point since he wasn't getting anywhere with the small talk he had attempted. "I saw you the other day and I know you overheard Eric and I talking. Stay away, and don't tell anyone, or it won't go well for you. I don't want you to get hurt, you seem like a nice girl."

"Are you threatening me? I don't intend telling anyone, I don't want to get mixed up in whatever it is you're involved in, and neither should you," replied Lily. "The black market isn't good, making money from desperate people isn't right at all."

Colin breathed a sigh of relief inwardly, she obviously hadn't picked up on anything. He and Eric were safe then, but they would have to be more careful in future, he didn't want Lily or anyone else hearing more of their conversation. He was just relieved it was he who saw Lily and not Eric. He would have to suggest to Eric they meet somewhere else so no one else could overhear them. Eric wouldn't have given her a friendly warning, he would just act. Eric really was a nasty piece of work and no one wanted to get on the wrong side of him.

Colin, having finished his business with Lily moved to another seat, as it was clear there was going to be no friendly conversation with her and certainly not after he had issued his warning. Lily was lost in thought and nearly missed the stop when they reached the hospital. Colin had to prod her to remind her to get off. She had been thinking of the threat that he had issued. What was it she had overheard that was worthy of a threat? She went back over the conversation in her mind, thinking there was something she must have missed, but couldn't find anything. Maybe they were so high up in the black market that if they were caught it would be a disaster. But that can't be right, she thought, because Eric had mentioned his boss, so he wasn't at the top of the chain. Maybe it was more than just black marketeering, something more criminal than that. She really couldn't think of what could be going on, so just left it at that, but there was a stirring of unease within her that she just couldn't shake. Something wasn't right but without knowing what it was there was nothing she could do. She would just do her best to keep out of their way in future.

Once at work, she continued through her day as normal. It was a busy shift with patients going to theatre and all the post op care they needed afterwards. There were new patients being admitted. Several patients were new having been hurt in last night's air raid. Fortunately, the porters assigned to the ward, taking patients to and from theatre were not Eric and Colin. Lily was relieved about this, she had no desire to come across them any time soon.

………

Lily was walking to her house when Joan rushed out to her. Seeing how distraught she looked Lily hurried over to her. "What's happened?" asked Lily, her mind immediately going to Arthur.

"It's Polly, she was on her way here yesterday, she met up with friends first to go to the pictures." Joan stopped, unable to carry on.

Lily with a bad feeling about this, put her hand on Joan's arm. "Slow down, and tell me exactly what happened," said Lily, keeping her voice quiet and calming.

"Polly, it's Polly," begun Joan, unable to continue.

"Why don't we go inside and I'll put the kettle on. You've clearly had a shock and some hot, sweet tea will help. Then you can tell me what happened," said Lily.

"No, no, there isn't time, we have to get to the hospital," replied Joan.

Lily had a feeling this was not going to end well, and said, "Ok, we can do that. Is Arthur ready? We can't leave him alone."

"Yes."

"Come on then, we'll get Arthur and then we'll go."

The two women went inside and helped Arthur to his feet. Lily was concerned to see Arthur in a worse state than usual. He was sat there ashen, and trembling. He was in a world of his own and showed no sign of recognising the two women. Lily went over to him and spoke soothingly, "It's ok Arthur, you're safe, we're just going to visit the hospital. Can you stand up." Lily took him by the arm and helped him stand.

They were soon at the hospital and Lily suggested going to see Matron, knowing she would have all the information needed, plus Joan and Arthur were in no fit state to be wandering around the hospital.

Lily knocked on the door and when the stern voice of Matron bade them enter she went in followed by her friends.

"Hello Matron, I'm here with my friends Joan and Arthur, they had a message that something happened to their daughter Polly last night and were to come here."

"Ah yes," said Matron, not relishing this conversation, but one that she was having all too many of these days. "Do sit down. Unfortunately, your daughter was caught up in the air raid last night. She and her friends were rushing to the shelter but didn't get there in time before the bombs started dropping. She was hit on the head by falling rubble from a collapsing building and knocked out. She was bought in unconscious from a severe head injury and unfortunately, there was nothing we could do. She died a couple of hours ago. One of her friends is here with a broken leg and collar bone and was able to tell us what happened. I'm so very sorry."

Joan gave a low moan, her face going a greyish colour at the news. Lily put her arm around her and held her close. Arthur begun repeating a nursery rhyme:

*"Polly put the kettle on,*
*Polly put the kettle on,*
*Polly put the kettle on and we'll all have tea."*

Matron stood up and came around her desk. She was used to seeing all sorts of reaction to grief, nothing surprised her anymore.

"I'm sorry, Arthur gets like this. He repeats nursery rhymes a lot. He was affected by shell shock in the Great War and has never recovered. All the bombs being dropped in this war have made him worse. He is very much in his own little world. I don't know how much he has taken in of what you just said," said Lily, by way of explanation.

"That's ok," said Matron, approaching Arthur. "Sir, listen to me, look at me," she continued, as Arthur was staring at the floor repeating the nursery rhyme under his breath. "Your wife needs you now. I'm very sorry I've had to give you such bad news. If you are to get through this time you need to help each other. I know this has come as a shock but you can get through this together."

Arthur made no response, continuing his repetition. Matron had no idea if he had even heard or understood what she had just said. "I'll send for a cup of tea for you, that will help, you have both had a dreadful shock."

She went to the door and caught a passing nurse, issuing her request. Very soon there was a knock and the nurse came in carrying a tray of tea for all of them. Matron handed them all a cup but Lily had to help Joan with hers as she was shaking so much.

"Come on," said Lily, "This will help you feel better." She held the cup to Joan's lips and Joan took a sip of the hot, sweet tea. Lily and Matron were relieved to see the colour start to return to her face. Matron held the cup for Arthur and tried to get him to sip his tea.

"Well done," said Matron, as Arthur began to sip his tea obediently.

When they had finished their tea she asked, "Would you like to see her?"

Joan started, and looked up, "Sorry, what did you say?" she gave her head a shake.

"I asked if you wanted to see your daughter. It might help accept what has happened. I know it can be difficult to take in at first, but some people find it helps if they can see the body."

"What do you mean, see the body? She is my daughter, not just a body," said Joan, annoyed at having her daughter's humanity taken away, or that is how it seemed to her. How could Matron speak in that way about Polly?

"I'm sorry, I didn't mean anything by it. Would you like to see your daughter," corrected Matron.

Joan thought about it, not knowing how to respond. To be honest she had no idea what she wanted to do. She was torn between wanting to see her daughter but not wanting to see her body. Matron had been right. She would just be looking at the body not at her daughter. Her daughter was no longer there and never would be again.

"I don't know what to do for the best," she said quietly.

"It can help," said Lily. "It can be difficult to take in at first when a loved one gets bad news like this, but seeing the body can help make it seem real."

"Ok then," said Joan. "But I'm not sure about Arthur."

"He can come as well, you never know it might help him. I don't think he should be left here on his own and being with a stranger would probably not be a good idea," said Matron.

Joan nodded her head and got to her feet. Matron lead the way and they followed her to the mortuary.

A body was laid out on the table, covered with a sheet. "I'll be outside waiting," said Matron, not wanting to intrude on their grief.

"Do you want me to stay? I can wait outside with Matron if you would rather be alone with her," queried Lily.

"No, please stay," said Joan, clinging on to Lily's arm.

Lily nodded and slowly pulled the sheet back that covered Polly. Joan gave a small moan and would have collapsed if it wasn't for Lily holding tightly on to her friend.

"No, no, no, this can't be happening. My Polly, she's too young. She can't die, this must be some awful mistake. She had her whole life ahead of her," cried Joan, pulling herself free from Lily's arms and clutching her daughter's body.

"She is so cold, please get her a blanket, she needs to get warm. We have to warm her up."

Lily tried to separate Joan from Polly, saying, "It won't help, Joan, she's gone. I'm so sorry but she isn't coming back."

"No that can't be right, she's just cold. She'll wake up in a minute if she warms up a bit."

"She isn't going to warm up Joan. She has gone."

"What happened? This can't be." Joan shook her head, trying to clear it, unable to take in what was happening.

Lily spoke quietly, "She got caught in the raid last night, she was hit by some falling rubble and suffered a severe head injury. It was too severe and she never recovered consciousness."

"Would she have suffered?" asked Joan, asking the question, but not sure she wanted the answer.

"No, she would have been unconscious," replied Lily.

Suddenly Joan let out an ear splitting scream and sank to the floor. Matron opened the door and came in on hearing the noise. She went to where Lily was kneeling beside her friend and holding her tight.

Arthur had just been stood there, motionless, while all this was taking place. Now, he bent down to his wife and touched her shoulder. Lily and Matron looked at each other. Was Arthur aware of what was happening after all? Had the scream from Joan made him act? Whatever it was they were encouraged by his response. They needed each other if they were to survive this. No one really knew though, if Arthur really had understood what had happened or if he was just reacting to his wife's distress.

"I've got you," said Lily, holding Joan in her arms while Joan continued to emit screams again and again.

"I'll call a doctor," said Matron quietly. Lily nodded in agreement.

Matron and Lily tried to get Joan and Arthur back to the office but Joan refused to leave her daughter on her own, convinced Polly would be lonely and frightened if she woke up and found herself alone.

The doctor, when he arrived, spoke quietly to Joan, "It's ok, she is well looked after here. We'll look after her now, you can leave her to us. Right now we need to get you back to Matron's room."

Somehow they managed to get Joan to her feet and with Matron and the doctor supporting her they managed to get her back to the office. Lily followed behind with a bewildered looking Arthur.

Back in the office, another cup of tea was ordered.

"I think you would benefit from a mild sedative," said the doctor to Joan. "It might be best if we kept an eye on you as well, just over night."

"No I can't. Arthur, he needs me, he won't cope without me. I have to be at home with him."

"It's ok doctor," said Lily, "I'll stay with them for the rest of the day and overnight. I'll look after them both."

"Well, I'm not sure," said the doctor, then seeing a nod from Matron changed his mind and said, "I suppose that would be acceptable, you're a nurse after all."

Joan was a bit calmer now, having had another cup of tea, which helped persuade the doctor as well. He gave Lily a bottle of tablets to give Joan one if it was necessary.

Somehow Lily managed to get Joan and Arthur on the bus and sat them down. Lily was starting to regret her decision to look after them. It was like looking after a couple of children and she wasn't sure how she would get them home on her own.

Colin got on the bus at the next stop and nodded to Lily before going to sit at the back. Lily, putting her past encounter with the porter behind her asked him to sit with her. If she was to coax them off the bus and back home she would need help. She was a bit surprised to see Colin because she never usually saw him on the same buses. What she didn't know was Matron being very concerned about how Lily would manage both Joan and Arthur had asked Colin to help, but not to make it obvious, just to be around in case of need.

Lily said, "I'm so glad to see you. These are my friends and neighbours, Joan and Arthur." She indicated her friends who were sat in the seat in front of her. She continued, "They have had a bit of a shock. Their daughter was killed in the raid last night and Joan has taken the news quite badly. We don't know how much Arthur has understood of the situation as he lives in his own little world ever since shell shock in the trenches of the Great War."

"Not a problem, I'm happy to help," said Colin, glad to be doing something to help as he felt a bit guilty at the threat he had issued to Lily before, but it needed to be done for her own safety, these were dangerous people and she needed to stay clear of them.

When the bus reached the appropriate stop he and Lily managed to get Joan and Arthur to their feet and off the bus. Colin, having a word with the driver had managed to persuade him to wait for them to get off in case it took a bit longer. The driver was happy to agree. Everyone helped each other in these terrible days and he had seen the pallor of Joan's face.

Between them they managed to get Joan and Arthur home when Colin said goodbye and left them to it.

Lily didn't know what to say as she sat with the couple. Joan was sat staring into space and Arthur was rocking and repeating nursery rhymes as usual. Lily thought they had, had enough tea at the hospital, they would be swimming in it if they had another cup. She felt sorry for the pair, who already had enough to cope with.

Joan's voice broke in on her thoughts, "Why did it have to happen? Why didn't she get to the shelter in time? Why did rubble have to hit her on the head from the collapsing building? Why didn't she come straight home instead of deciding to go to the pictures? Why did her friend have to survive and not her?" All these questions rattled off like bullets from Joan's mouth.

"I don't know," replied Lily, reaching over and touching Joan's arm. There were no answers to these questions and all the other questions going around and round in Joan's mind at that moment. "I don't think anyone can answer those questions except Polly, and she isn't here."

"Polly, Polly, my beautiful girl. She was too young. She had her whole life ahead of her." Joan broke down into sobs at this point.

Lily held her while she cried and cried. Eventually she settled down with just the occasional catch in her throat. Lily continued to hold her, wanting to be of some comfort to her friend but at the same time feeling helpless that she couldn't do more for her.

In the meantime, Arthur continued sitting rocking, as if nothing untoward was happening. He seemed completely oblivious to his wife's sobbing as he continued to repeat his nursery rhymes:

*"Polly put the kettle on,*
*Polly put the kettle on,*
*Polly put the kettle on we'll all have tea."*

Lily was relieved that Arthur, in his own world, didn't have to face the grief that Joan was enduring at this time.  That was the only comfort that could be achieved at this present moment in time.

"Maybe you should go and lie down and try to get some sleep," said Lily. "You must have a headache from all that crying."

"I don't think I'll ever sleep again," said Joan.

"Of course you will. Sleep is probably the best thing for you. At least you'll get some relief from the pain."

"Yes, but I'll wake up and face the same pain again and again. Will it ever go away? I can't stand it."

"I know, but it will get easier. Time is a great healer," said Lily, hiding behind trite sayings, not knowing how to help her friend. She didn't know why she said it really because she had seen in her own life that time did not heal the pain caused by grief. She was relieved though that Joan was talking, something her mother had never done.

At that moment the siren went off, "Come on, we have to get to the shelter," said Lily wearily. They were all getting fed up of the sound of that siren going off. The shelter was becoming their home, with its damp, musty smell. It was not built for comfort but practicality. They almost lived there these days though, so were getting used to it, they had no choice really.

"Why bother going to the shelter, we might as well stay where we are. If a bomb has our name on it then so be it. What does it matter?" questioned Joan.

"You don't mean that," said Lily sharply. "Polly wouldn't want you to give up, you know that."

"She isn't here though is she, she'll never be again, so what does it matter?"

"I won't let you give up. I still need my friend. I'm here for you and you will get through it."

"Like your mum did you mean," cried Joan, hitting below the belt in her grief. Lily took a sharp intake of breath at this statement.

"I'm sorry," said Joan, regretting her words. "That was wrong of me to bring that up. I didn't mean to hurt you. I don't know why I said it really."

"It's all right," said Lily. "You are grieving and weren't thinking about what you're saying. I understand. Come on, we really must get to the shelter before the bombing starts. I can hear the sound of planes nearby."

Joan stood up and between them they got Arthur to his feet and made their slow way to the shelter in the back garden.

## Chapter Six

Lily was walking past a store cupboard when she heard voices whispering.

"No Colin we have to act now, the bosses are going to send someone else in to look at what we are doing, if we do not do something."

"What can we do though, we haven't had anyone in who can give us the information to pass on," said Colin. "This is a very sensitive issue, we can't just get what they want straight away."

"You are not pulling your weight. You have to take more chances, ask more questions or else," said Eric menacingly.

"I'm doing my best but can't get anything if there is nothing to get. Besides, we had to leave things a bit because I thought we had been overheard." Colin was trying to talk himself out of trouble here. The tone and words from Eric boded ill. He knew how dangerous Eric could be if crossed and didn't relish getting into trouble with him or those higher up the chain.

Lily stood still. Not again, she thought. Why did it always have to be she who heard these conversations between the porters. She had put out of her mind the conversation she had overheard last time. She hurried past not wanting to hear anymore. Colin seemed to be in trouble for some reason but she didn't want to know.

What with the death of Polly she was spending a lot of time with Joan and Arthur at the moment. Joan was starting to deal with it but was still grieving and leaning a lot on her friend. Arthur, as usual was in his own little world and she didn't know how much he had really understood of what had happened. For the first few days after the dreadful news, Lily had spent all of her free time with her friends as Joan was in pieces, in no fit state to take care of herself or Arthur. Gradually, Joan had started to take in the news and accept the tragedy. She recognised that she was only going through what so many were facing in these dark days. All she wanted to do now was talk about Polly, usually about her as a little girl. Polly had been fun loving, an extrovert, always out playing with friends. She had especially enjoyed skipping and playing hopscotch with others. She never stopped chatting, a right little chatterbox as Joan described her. She would tell Joan all about her day at school, nothing got missed out. She would even tell of the trouble she got into for talking in class, which was a daily occurrence. Joan always gave a small smile as she recalled these fond memories. Lily was only too willing to listen to Joan talking of Polly's childhood. It would be cathartic for Joan to talk like this.

Lily was also thinking of her upcoming visit from Ted and Winnie which was due to happen the next day.

Ted and Winnie turned up at the agreed time having had no problem with buses due to bomb damage.

Lily let them in with a smile, happy to see them again. "Come in," she said. "I'm so pleased to see you. Sit down anywhere."

Ted and Winnie looked around the room and noticed the lack of photos of family. They looked at each other, it looked as if their suspicions were right that her parents were somehow involved in the serious, sad look on her face.

"How have you been since we saw you last?" asked Winnie.

"I've been spending a lot of time with my friend next door," replied Lily, going on to tell them about Joan and Arthur and their grief.

"That's so tragic," said Winnie with tears in her eyes. "I really hope things improve for them soon, they sound as if they have already been through a lot without this on top of everything."

"It's Joan more than Arthur I worry about," said Lily, "she is having to deal with it on her own which isn't how it should be. In normal circumstances they would deal with it together but as things stand she is alone. I can't be there with her all the time, I have to work, although I spend a lot of time with them when I am off duty. Anyway," she said changing the subject, "take a seat and I'll bring the tea through."

When they were all seated and sipping the tea Winnie said, "This is a nice house you have here. I love this oak furniture and the comfy chairs look nice as well, but I can't help noticing how bare the mantelpiece looks with no photos of family." She recognised straightaway she had gone too far as she saw a stiffening in Lily. Before that sentence Lily had been relaxed and happy in the company of her new friends.

Ted, wanting to change the subject and get rid of the awkwardness in the atmosphere said, "Winnie, my darling…"

He was unable to finish as Winnie looking suspicious said, "Don't blinking darling me man, when you call me darling I know you are up to something and trying to get around me, well it won't work this time, I know all your tricks after all these blinking years together." She picked up her handbag and down it came on Ted's head.

Ted rubbed his head pretending to be mortally wounded, "Ouch that hurt woman, that bag of yours will kill me one of these days."

"Oh will it," said Winnie, lifting her bag up again and bringing it down on him.

Lily was watching the exchange with a smile on her face, these two really were a couple of comedians. She was so glad to have them in her life.

Ted and Winnie looked at each other seeing Lily relax again and the smile appear on her face. They had achieved the outcome they had wanted.

"Are you two ever serious," asked Lily genuinely interested.

"Of course we are, you don't think we could keep this up all day, every day do you? We love to have fun but life isn't always a bed of roses, and these days you never know what will happen, any day could be our last if a bomb has our name on it.  Look at what happened to your friends next door, it could be us next."

"Too true," said Ted.  "Old Hitler has a lot to answer for, if only he hadn't got greedy and decided to take over Europe we might not be in this mess now. He obviously has his sights on us next, but we are too strong for that, we'll fight him to the bitter end and we will win."

It surprised Lily how thoughtful and deep this couple were, showing an intelligence she hadn't expected from them. They were always joking and teasing each other, it never seemed to end.

"If you ever get fed up with each other Ted is always welcome here," she said, knowing this would cause mayhem again. Sure enough it came.

"What do you blinking mean by that exactly?" asked Winnie with an edge to her voice.

"I wouldn't want Ted to be stuck for somewhere to go," said Lily trying to get out of the hole she was digging for herself.

"You mean you want him for yourself. You are trying to steal my blinking man," Without further ado Winnie lifted her handbag and brought it down on Lily's head. This is resulted in much laughter from Ted and Winnie while a bemused Lily looked on before joining in the laughter.

Ted and Winnie were definitely proving to be good for Lily and they hoped in time that sad look would leave her so that she blossomed into the person she was meant to be.

"I was wondering if you could give us your husband's name and address as we would like to write to him so he knows we are looking out for you. If he knows that, it might take that worry off his mind so he can concentrate on getting the job done," said Ted.

"I'm sure he would be pleased to hear from you," said Lily, writing on a piece of paper and giving it to the couple.

"You belong to us now, we'll look out for you and we're here if you need us," replied Winnie.

"Thank you, that means a lot to me. There has never really been anyone there who I could turn to."

"If you want to talk we're good listeners," said Winnie putting a hand on Lily's arm in a gesture of support and comfort.

"Maybe one day," said Lily, knowing instinctively that she could trust these two with her life, they wouldn't let her down. She knew she had made lifelong friends with them and was so grateful for the time Ted had spent on the ward she was working on and that they had cared enough to want to befriend her.

"Earth to Lily," said Ted, as Lily had a faraway look in her eyes as indeed she was.

"Sorry," said Lily. "I was just thinking it was good that you were on the ward where I was working and I'm so grateful for the kindness and concern you've shown me."

"Don't get all soppy on us," said Winnie, giving Lily's arm a squeeze.

Lily's eyes filled with tears that ran unchecked down her cheeks. The kindness of this pair was too much for the vulnerable, hurting Lily. She had never got over the effect her childhood had on her and this pair were bringing it all up.

"Ay don't cry love," said Winnie, drawing her into a hug and letting her cry it all out. "Everything will be ok, we're here for you."

"I'm so sorry," said Lily trying to speak amidst the sobs. "I've never had anyone to talk to before and I'm not used to such kindness."

Winnie's heart ached for this young lady whose heart had so obviously been broken during her formative years. She wondered if Lily would ever be whole again, but if it was within her power she would help in any way she could. It wasn't in her to leave someone who was so obviously suffering.

"Take your time, just tell us what you're comfortable saying," said Winnie when the sobbing started to cease.

Lily moved away and looked at Winnie through red rimmed eyes from all the crying she had done.

"All right, I'll tell you my story, I think I'm ready for you to know what happened. I trust you both." Lily proceeded to tell the whole tragic tale.

Ted and Winnie listened without saying a word but the pain they felt for this young woman was reflected in their faces. She had gone through so much, so young and now they understood the serious, sad look that was always on her face. She had never had any real childhood, being forced to grow up at such a young age. They wished there was something they could do, but nothing could make up for what she had gone through. All they could do was be friends and bring some of the love and laughter into her life that she had missed out on.

"We're so sorry poppet," said Winnie, speaking for both of them. "You're not alone anymore you have a lovely husband and son, and we're here for you."

"I'm worried if anything happens to Jack I'll be like my mother was and then I'll be useless to Bobby."

"You're not your mum, you're Lily who is a strong person who has so much to give. You're a good nurse and a good friend to your neighbours supporting them through their struggles. We'll be here if the worst does happen, you won't face it alone," said Ted.

"Thank you, but how can I be sure? No one knows how they will react to grief until it happens."

"That's true but most people are able to move through it although they never forget their loved one. For your mum to have such a severe reaction that she got stuck in is unusual. You need to think about the future poppet. Think of your son he needs you," said Winnie. "You need to put the past behind you, you can't change what happened but it is over. I know you have paid a high price for what happened, but focus now on the present. You're no longer alone dealing with anything that comes along."

"Thank you," said Lily again. "I really appreciate your kindness and concern for me."
"Anytime," said Ted.

# Chapter seven

*Dear Jack,*

*Ted and Winnie came around again for a cup of tea today. They are such a nice couple. You would like them I know.  I found myself telling them about my mum and what my childhood was like. They were very reassuring and are so sure I won't be like mum if anything happened to you. I hope they're right. I really value their friendship and feel I'm not alone anymore. I'm starting to see them as the parents I never had.*

*I had a picture from Bobby again today. I miss him so much, I long to see him again. He is growing up fast and I am missing out on so much of his childhood. According to Megan he is writing much better and reads to her. I should be seeing that not Megan and Hugh. He is our son, not theirs. They're seeing all these crucial stages of development. When will this war end? If it wasn't for Hitler we'd be together as a family and would be able to delight in our son's development together as his parents, just as it should be.*

*Sorry for rambling on like this, I just miss you both and long for us to be a family again. Don't worry about me, I'm all right. Anyway I must close for now as I need to get ready for work.*

*Much love to you as always*
*Lily.*


..........

Jack read the letter and felt a pang of nostalgia for the happy times before the war when they were together as a family. He too, longed for this war to be over so they could be together again. As things stood it looked as if it would be a long time before that would happen, there was still no let up in the bombings of London and other important cities. Daily they were up in the air and coming down again not knowing which of their comrades had "bought it". There was always someone who didn't come back. So far he was lucky and had come back in one piece but so many friends had lost their lives, been badly injured or were shot down and taken prisoner by the Germans.

Jack opened the next letter he had received and began to read.

*Dear Jack,*

*I hope you don't mind me writing to you like this. You don't know me but me and my husband have become friends with your Lily. Our names are Ted and Winnie. We got to know Lily while Ted was in hospital and since then have met up a couple of times for a good old cup of tea. When Ted first mentioned her to me I thought he was flirting with the nurses again so I gave him what for, then when he explained to me I saw for myself and wanted to befriend this sad, serious person. She told us of her upbringing recently which moved us to tears, although we waited until we got home to let the tears flow. It is such a sad story and I know one of her main concerns is that she will turn out like her*

Jack stopped reading for a moment to laugh
at this vision of this woman knocking people over
the head with the handbag. He had heard this
from Lily so already knew about it, but it did
sound funny all over again coming from Winnie.
He went back to the letter:



Jack read through the letter a couple of
times. Yes, his Lily would be fine with these two,
they seemed like a lot of fun and at the same time
were very caring and had taken his serious, sad
wife under their wing. He felt something lift
inside him, feeling a lessening of the burden and
worry for Lily, who, if anything happened to him
would be all alone. He wondered when he would
next get a pass as he longed to meet the couple
who had taken his Lily under their wing. They
sounded like a fun couple, just what Lily needed.

He hoped they would take that serious, sad look from his wife's face. He had hoped to do that when they married but it hadn't happened, the wounds went too deep. He must reply to Ted and Winnie he decided, but first he must respond to his beloved Lily.

*Dear Lily darling,*

*It was wonderful as always to hear from you. You are my life my darling and mean the world to me. I love you with all my heart, both you and Bobby, and I miss you both very much. I wish this war would finish so we could be together again but things don't show any signs of easing off at all. We are still being kept busy and showing no signs of being allowed a pass or any proper leave. We are all very tired but still have to go up and fight to bring an end to this attack on our dear country.*

*I am sorry to hear about Polly, but am pleased you can be of some comfort to Joan and Arthur, however little that may be. Please give them my love and tell them how sorry I am.*

*I enjoyed reading your account of Ted and Winnie, what a laugh they seem to be. I am so pleased you have become friends with them. From what you say you won't be short of laughter that's for sure. It will be good for you to have some laughter in your life. I am pleased that they are there for you in case anything should happen to me, although I pray to God it won't. I would do anything to spare you that pain if I could but obviously in these days of war nothing is guaranteed. We regularly lose men up in the air. We* come back not knowing who else has made it and wondering what has happened to the others.

When you next write could you enclose one of Bobby's pictures. I miss him so much and it would be something of his to keep looking at and a reminder of what we are fighting for. We must rid this world of the Nazis and all that they stand for so that our children may live free and safe.

Missing you and longing for the time we can be together again, to feel you in my arms. How good that would be, and I am longing to meet Ted and Winnie. Never doubt my love for you, you are my life and I long to be back with you all the time.

Love and kisses
Your Jack


Dear Ted and Winnie,

Thank you for your lovely letter. I was so pleased to hear from you. I have heard about you from Lily but enjoyed hearing from you directly. Thank you for befriending my lovely wife, she means the world to me, but hasn't had an easy life. She needs someone like you both, someone who can bring love and laughter into her situation. As you know she hasn't had much of that in the past and I would love that to change. She deserves better than she has had so far.

Life is so uncertain and fragile at the moment with this war, no one knows what will happen next. Every time I go up in the plane I realise just what a fragile hold on life we have. I don't know if I will come back down in one piece. Every day I am seeing friends die, shot to pieces in the air and one day it could be my *turn if I am being realistic and I need to know Lily is going to be all right and taken care of if the worst should happen. Now she has you in her life I am not so worried about Lily as I can tell you care deeply about her and will look after her if necessary. I don't for one minute think she will turn out like her mother but it reassures me knowing you will be there with her.*

*You seem like a fun loving couple and hopefully one day I will get the chance to meet you, although I am not sure I like the idea of my wife being hit over the head with a handbag! Thanks for telling me that, it definitely made my day brighter.*

*Please write back, I would love to hear from you.*

*All my best wishes to you both,*
*Jack.*


. . . . . . . . . .


Ted and Winnie read Jack's letter and tears came to their eyes, it was such a heartfelt letter. He quite clearly adored Lily and wanted her to have a better life. A life with much love and laughter in it. Well they would make sure she did, that is what they wanted for Lily as well. They were coming to regard Lily as the daughter they never had, but longed for. If that was one regret they had in life, it was the sadness of not having children, they would have loved a daughter like Lily. Although she was so serious and sad they were discovering that underneath the real Lily lay, someone who loved a laugh and cared deeply about others. They could see that with the way she was looking after her neighbours during their time of mourning for their lost daughter. There was no way Lily would turn out like her mother they could see that, even though she couldn't. It made them sad to think of the neglect she had suffered growing up, nothing could change what had happened in the past but they were determined to change her present and future. Yes, Lily would have the mothering she had missed out on.

. . . . . . . .

Lily read Jack's letter with a smile on her face. She was glad he liked the sound of Ted and Winnie for she was very fond of the older couple and was beginning to see them as her adopted parents. Although an adult now with a family of her own she still longed for parents to turn to and share her life with, maybe as a result of missing out on that when she was growing up. Yes, that funny couple were definitely like parents to her, they were bringing love and laughter into her life.

It was becoming obvious to everyone who knew and cared about Lily that Ted and Winnie were having such a big impact on her life. She was smiling more, starting to chat more and was generally looking happier than they had ever seen her. Matron was so pleased she had gone with her instincts and let the couple meet and befriend her.

These changes were showing in her nursing as well, she was becoming a better nurse, although she had always been a very good nurse. She still had a serious, sad look about her and maybe that would never completely go but things were definitely changing.

………

*Dear Jack,*

*Thank you so much for writing to us. We loved hearing from you and hope to keep in contact with you and if God is willing to meet one day. You won't recognise Lily when you next see her, she is really starting to blossom out and is much readier with a smile and a laugh. She still has that serious, sad look but is starting to open up and have a joke with us. We love to see this and it's what we wanted to happen when we first decided we wanted to befriend her. We are sorry to tell you she has been hit over the head with the handbag again, although we are sure you would agree with the necessity of it as she was getting too comfortable with Ted and flirting a bit. I couldn't allow that to happen now could I? I am sure you will agree that such a punishment was necessary to keep her in line! It might reassure you to know that when she gets the handbag treatment she laughs as much as we do, which definitely makes it worthwhile in our eyes. When we first met her we tried to manipulate the conversation so the handbag was needed just to try to bring a smile and laughter to her. We are finding it comes more readily to her now than it did, and sometimes she is the one who starts the jokes and laughter. She has a strong sense of humour hidden underneath that serious exterior*

*Love to you*
*Ted and Winnie.*

Jack read the short letter with a smile on his face. He laughed out loud at hearing his wife was getting the handbag for flirting with Ted, and agreed she deserved it. These two were really a pair of jokers and he couldn't wait to meet them. They were definitely doing Lily good if they were able to break through that exterior to get to who she really was underneath. He had never managed to break down the barriers she had built up around herself but these two had and he was more than grateful to them.

*Dear Lily,*

*I just heard from Ted and Winnie and they tell me you were knocked over the head with the handbag because of flirting with Ted. You definitely deserved it! I had a good laugh over it my darling. I am so pleased you are coming out of your shell and starting to laugh and joke a bit with these two. They sound a right hoot. I can't wait to meet them. I am so pleased you see them as the parents you never had. They would have made wonderful parents, it's so sad they never had that opportunity, any child would have been lucky to have them. I'm so pleased they have come into your life my darling as you deserve something good to happen and building a network of people around you is a good start. Everything will be all right, I just know it.*

*I love you so much my darling girl. You and our little Bobby. I can't wait until I am next able to see you both but there seems no sign of things settling down at the moment. The Jerries are as active as ever as you will know with all the air raids.*

*Much love*
*Jack xxxxxxx*

*Dear Lily,*

*I'm enclosing the latest drawing from Bobby as usual with this letter. He is such a good boy, a pleasure to have around. Every morning he goes out and collects the eggs from the hens. He does this on his own now without us needing to prompt or supervise him. He loves to help me in the kitchen and I encourage this as much as possible.*

*He is growing very quickly and outgrowing the clothes he has. Don't worry though, we are more than happy to buy him some new ones. You know he is a son to us. He enjoys playing with friends and often has friends around or is going to them. Don't worry about him, everything is fine and he is more than happy with us.*

*Yours*
*Megan and Hugh.*

Lily read this latest letter with a smile. She loved getting these brief updates from Megan and Hugh, they were very good about keeping her involved with what was happening in her son's life. They were definitely a very special couple, not many were kept so involved in the lives of their children. She must send some money though to buy Bobby the new clothes he needed. How she wished she could visit, she would love to meet this couple and of course she would be overjoyed to see her son whom she missed so much. She resented that another couple were seeing him develop and grow when it should be her seeing this and rejoicing with Jack.

## Chapter eight

"What's got you so happy?" asked Grace, the ward sister. "It's not often we see you with a smile on your face."

"I had a lovely time with Ted and Winnie yesterday. They're so funny."

"That explains a lot," said Grace. She was so pleased to see Lily looking so alive and happy. Ted and Winnie were obviously good for her. "What were they up to this time?"

"Winnie gave me the handbag treatment for agreeing with Ted when they were arguing over what was women's work. He was complaining about women working in munitions factories and the land girls doing farming and saying it was wrong for women to be doing that work. Winnie was getting all feminist on the subject so I felt I had to stick up for poor Ted. Winnie took exception to this and knocked me over the head, said I should be sticking up for her and for all women. Her view was that all women are capable of doing men's work they just need to be given a chance."

Grace laughed. "You know, I agree with her. I think this war is proving that women are as capable as men and should have equal rights when it comes to employment. I think you'll find things change after the war in the area of work for women."

Lily agreed with Grace and then went about her work on the ward. She shared a friendly word with the men as she went around the ward taking blood pressure and pulse and making sure post-operative patients were comfortable.

It was later when she was going on her break to get some fresh air that she overheard Eric and Colin. They seemed to be arguing about something.

"You will do what I say," said Eric furiously.

"I don't think I can do what you ask," replied Colin.

"You will, or I will have to take this further and you will not like that. You better watch your back in future, you will never know when it is going to come or by whom."

"I can't do something that will mean people getting hurt," said Colin.

"You will do as you are told. You are doing it for the greater good you know that. We all have to play our part in bringing down the enemy."

Lily hurried by, not wanting to hear what was being said. They were obviously involved in something more than the black market but she didn't want to know. It seemed as if Colin didn't want to be involved though. She remembered how Colin had helped with Joan when she needed to get her and Arthur home after finding out Polly had died. He had been so kind and helpful, she couldn't have managed without him. She found it hard to believe that he would be involved in anything illegal. He had seemed a good guy.

It was when she was back on the ward that the summons came. Matron was asking to see her, she panicked at first wondering what she had done that warranted a call from Matron like this. She quickly checked to make sure she was decent then went to the office inwardly quaking.

Matron was lost in thought when Lily arrived. She had been thinking of the first time she had called Lily to her office which had also been to give her bad news. At that time she was telling her of her grandparents death in a car accident. It had been the first time she had really met Lily and like everyone else had been struck by the serious, sad look on her face. Lily had barely shown any emotion on being told the news. This had come as a surprise to Matron who was expecting, well she wasn't sure what she had expected but not this blankness. It was as if Lily had built such a wall around herself that nothing could touch her. The next time she had seen Lily in her office was when her mother died. She had a heart attack and died the day war was announced. Matron, not knowing the background was not to know that the announcement of war had been too much for Flo, it took her back to the last war breaking out when her husband had been called up never to return. Somewhere in her disturbed mind she had been aware of what had happened but just couldn't face it. Again on that occasion, Lily had shown no emotion, she just continued as if nothing had happened which struck Matron as distinctly odd.

Matron was brought back to the present with a knock at the door. She didn't know how Lily would react to the news she was just about to give her.

"Enter," said the stern voice of Matron when Lily knocked.

Lily entered, hoping her fear didn't show on her face.

"Ah Lily, take a seat," said Matron in a kind voice. She had seen how much Lily had started to open up and be less serious and sad thanks to the influence of Ted and Winnie. They had clearly been good for her, but things were about to change and Matron hated what she was about to tell Lily and take the smile off her face. She was going to need her friends now more than ever.

"Lily I received a phone call a short while ago. I'm so sorry to have to tell you but your husband Jack has been injured and is in a hospital on the coast. I don't know what the situation is at the moment so I have no idea how bad it is," she said gently.

Lily paled at the news. No, this couldn't be happening, not Jack, this was exactly what she had been worried about all along.  Matron left her seat and went around the desk perching on the edge of it.

"Now, don't think the worst," said Matron. "We don't know how bad he is. I can ring them back and find out more if they will tell me. I only knew this because the matron there is an old friend of mine, we trained together, so she phoned to let me know instead of sending you a telegram."

"Please if you would phone back I'd be very grateful," said Lily in a small voice. The serious, sad look was back on her face with worry and fear added to it.

"No problem," said Matron, patting Lily's arm.

She picked up the phone to make the call. "Hello, is that Eve," she asked on being put through to the Matron there. "I've got Lily with me now and she asked me to find out more information if you can give it…. Yes, yes, ok… So that is all then… yes that's fine, I'll tell her, that should at least put her mind at rest. She'll be there as soon as she can, thank you so much Eve, it is good of you to let us know." Matron put the phone down and turned to Lily's frightened face.

"It's ok you don't need to look so scared," said Matron reassuringly. "He has a badly broken leg and some burns to his hands, but other than that he'll be fine when he has recovered from his injuries. He had a bang on the head but it wasn't serious." Matron was relieved not to be giving worse news to Lily. It could have been so much worse. That was the problem with the current events in the world, too often she was breaking bad news and she hated it. It was the worst part of the job.

She watched Lily carefully, waiting for a reaction and sure enough it came as the tears fell. Lily didn't really know why she was crying as it seemed Jack was going to be ok, but it was a relief to know that. Injured yes, but he would recover although it might take time. There was still a part of her that couldn't help thinking he would go downhill and she would lose him, after all he had a head injury, maybe the effects would be seen later. You never could tell with head injuries.

"He'll be all right," said Matron as if she could read Lily's thoughts. "You, of course, can take time off to go down there and be with him. You can take as much time as you need. Don't come back until he is fully recovered. We can manage without you and your place is with your husband."

Lily sniffed and wiped her eyes before saying, "Thank you Matron, I really appreciate this. Hopefully I won't be off too long."

"Don't worry about that, the hospital will be fine without you for a few weeks. Your place is with your husband now, nursing him back to health. Now go."

Lily stood up and left the hospital with a heavy heart. What would she find when she got down to Jack. Part of her was still worried in spite of Matron's reassurances, only being there with him would really be able to allay her fears. After all the hospital could have been playing it down not wanting to give the full horror over the phone. She was a nurse, she knew how things worked. She needed to write a brief note to Ted and Winnie to let them know what was happening and she must drop in on Joan before leaving. There seemed to be so many things to do and her mind was all muddled up, she couldn't think straight.

She got home and quickly packed a few things then scribbled a note for Ted and Winnie. She would post it on the way to catch the train. On her way out she knocked on Joan's door. Joan was surprised to see her friend as she knew she was working, but one look at her face told her something was very wrong.

"Come in, what is it?" asked Joan, ushering her friend inside.

"I can't stop. I'm on my way to Jack. He's been injured and is currently in hospital on the coast."

"Oh no, how bad is it?" Joan, well aware of Lily's fears was concerned for her friend.

"He has a broken leg and some burns, he also sustained a minor head injury but they're not worried, they say he'll be fine. I just need to get there and see for myself. I won't relax until I know for sure that he'll be ok. I know what hospitals are like they don't give very bad news over the phone."

"I'm so sorry I really hope Jack will be fine and please remember you are not alone in this, you have me and you also have Ted and Winnie. We'll get you through this, whatever the situation."

"Thanks Joan, I really needed to hear that. Well I should get off now if I want to get down there today. You know how slow the trains can be these days with air raids and bomb damage everywhere."

Lily hurriedly left and rushed to catch the train that would take her to Jack, still worried about what she would find when she got there.


……..


Lily walked into the hospital, inwardly quaking at what she would discover. Someone took her to Matron's office. Matron was quick to put her mind at rest. Jack really would be fine in time. His leg would mend although he might always have a bit of a limp as it was a bad break. The burns would heal in time and the head injury really wasn't of any significance. Matron had heard about Lily from her friend who had phoned her back after Lily had left so she wasn't surprised by the serious, sad face and wanted to allay her fears straight away.

Lily was taken to the ward where Jack was. As soon as she saw him she rushed up to him. She so wanted to give him a cuddle but it would have been too difficult and painful for Jack who was lying there with his leg in plaster, hands and arms dressed and a bandage around his head.

"Oh my darling, I'm so glad to see you. I was really worried when I got the news. I needed to see for myself that you were all right," cried Lily. "They told me about your leg and burns to your hands. How bad is it?"

"They have said it will take time, and I might have a permanent limp but I'll be back flying in no time. It takes more than that to get rid of me," replied Jack.

"Thank God!" said Lily, her mind slightly relieved now she could see her husband for herself.

"I have missed you so much, but I wish we were meeting under different circumstances."

"I've missed you as well, your letters aren't enough, I've longed to see you and cursed Hitler from here to eternity for keeping us apart," said Lily.

"We're together now at least. How long have we got before you have to be back at the hospital?" asked Jack.

"As long as I need. Matron said to stay until you're completely recovered."

"Great, we must make the most of it," said Jack, with a grin.

"Maybe when you're out of here we should take the opportunity to go and visit Bobby. I'm sure Megan and Hugh would be pleased to meet us and I don't want Bobby forgetting who we are," said Lily who secretly feared her darling son would forget his real parents. She knew that he had photos of them that Megan and Hugh were showing him regularly and they read her letters to him but he had been so young when he left home and the only contact had been through Megan and Hugh. How much did he really understand of the situation that kept him from his parents or did he think they didn't want him?

"Sounds a good plan," said Jack, who shared the same concerns as Lily in regard to their small son.

"At the moment let's concentrate on getting you better and out of here," said Lily. She longed to know just how bad the burns were but because of the thick dressings she couldn't see anything, maybe she should try to speak to a doctor, but then what would they tell her, she wasn't a nurse here just a relative. "Are you in much pain?" she asked, the nurse in her showing through.

"Quite a bit, but the painkillers help," said Jack. Oh how he longed to give his wife a cuddle but he couldn't, it would be too painful for his hands and moving his leg was difficult with the cast on it. The cuddle would have to wait a while until he was much better.

"Do you remember what happened?" asked Lily, wanting to know every detail.

"No," replied Jack. That wasn't strictly true, but he didn't want Lily to know the full horror of it. He remembered clearly as the Messerschmitt 109 had been directly above him when they had sent the shots reigning down. The fear he had felt and the smell as the plane had burst into flames starting in the tail was forever engraved in his mind. He had immediately turned back and hoped he could get down before the whole plane went up in flames then he would be a goner. All sorts of thoughts went through his mind, primarily concerning Lily and Bobby. Bobby who would never remember his father for he was too young to remember. How would Lily react to the news? Would she be like her mum as she had always feared or would she come through it with the help of her friends. Would it be a quick, merciful death or would it be a painful, protracted death. The flames leapt and danced as they took over the plane and he had no choice but to bail out and hope for the best.

He managed to free himself from the cockpit and pull himself out and jumped. At first he couldn't get the parachute to open and he knew real fear, he was too high up to hope to survive a jump, but then it opened and he slowly sailed down. It was just like he was floating on the clouds and at any other time would have been magical but in these tense times all he knew was fear. He was at the mercy of the enemy who could easily fire at him and that would be it if they hit him or the parachute. They would be talking about him back at base as someone who had bought it and then they would move on to another topic, not giving him a second thought. It always seemed callous but was their only way of surviving the fear, knowing they would have to go up again as they had a job to do. They couldn't allow fear to get in the way or the war would be lost. Jack knew how lucky he was, it could have been so much worse. His injuries could have been more severe and life changing or he could have been shot down over enemy territory and taken prisoner. How long would it have taken before Lily found out he was a prisoner? What agonies would she go through on hearing he was missing. It didn't bear thinking about and he kept his thoughts to himself, definitely not to be shared with his wife.

..........

Eric and Colin were talking in their usual place, which Eric deemed to be safe as it was a quiet part of the hospital with few people walking by. He didn't know that Lily had on two occasions overheard them for Colin hadn't told him, wanting to keep her safe.

"We have to find out information from somewhere about the military hospitals," said

Eric. "Pressure is being put on me and they want someone in place in one of them to talk to the patients to try and get information about what is going to happen."

"How do we do that?" asked Colin.

"I was thinking you would be the best placed to get a job there, then you would feedback to me what is happening so I can pass it on. I am unhappy about sending someone in who is unknown. You could find out where that husband of that nurse is. You know the one, she is always looking so sad and serious. If you went to that hospital you could get information from him."

"Wouldn't that look a bit odd if I suddenly turned up there? She would recognise me straight away."

"Are you disobeying an order?" questioned Eric in a menacing tone. "It will go badly for you if you are."

"No, no of course not, I wouldn't you know that," said Colin quickly. "I just meant she would know me and might start asking awkward questions as to why I've suddenly turned up there. I think it is better to send someone who she doesn't know. You must know someone in the network who could go and could be trusted to do as requested."

"You've got a point I suppose," said Eric grudgingly. He hated to admit that Colin was right in this instance. He liked to be top dog and didn't like anyone questioning an order that he had given.

Colin breathed a sigh of relief, he really didn't want Lily starting to ask awkward questions, she had already heard too much, but fortunately hadn't put two and two together. If he turned up there she might just do the maths and come up with the right answer and he wasn't ready for that – not yet! He still had work to do.

"I will ask Bruce, he is a good one, very loyal, I can trust him to help." Eric said, having given it some thought. If truth be told he didn't really want Colin to go, he wasn't sure how much he could really trust him. He seemed too argumentative at times, not accepting his authority. Yes, it was much better having Colin there where he could keep a close watch on him. He didn't really know what it was about Colin but there was something. There was nothing obvious that said Colin wasn't to be trusted just a gut instinct. He would deal with Colin if necessary. Maybe it would be a good idea to have someone following him, watching his every move. Yes, that is what he would do. He felt a bit better having made that decision. He would soon find out if Colin was a traitor or totally committed to the cause.

Colin at the same time was thinking about his position. Eric seemed to be stepping things up and was showing openly a suspicion of him, he would have to tread carefully, he couldn't afford to get found out and his true loyalties exposed. That would be too dangerous in these times. Somehow he had to find a way to show Eric he could be trusted and was very committed to the cause. He had to be seen as being above suspicion. Too much time had been spent trying to find out the information his superiors required and gaining Eric's trust for it to fall apart now. He was highly experienced but so was Eric. Eric was automatically suspicious of everyone but Colin had hoped to have earned his trust by now. He couldn't afford for the truth to come out yet, he still needed more information.

"Is there anything I can do?" asked Colin, wanting to be seen to be cooperating.

"No, nothing just continue as you are, keeping a close eye on what is happening outside, keep your ear to the ground and continue passing messages. You are my link with the network so no one knows who I am, the same as no one knows who my superiors are or where they are," replied Eric, mellowing a bit towards Colin now he had decided what to do.

Colin wanted to give the salute but felt that might be going too far and arouse Eric's suspicions further. He would have to watch his back as he was sure Eric would be keeping a close eye on him. He wasn't totally convinced that Eric was being truthful when he said only he knew Eric and was the go between. He would start to vary his routes used to see if he was being followed and start going some very obscure ways that would show him if anyone was on his trail.

Colin and Eric went their separate ways soon after. They were not friends, just doing a job. They both knew that in this work they couldn't afford to make friends, it was important to avoid suspicion. The results would mean death if they were discovered. It was imperative therefore, that they were very careful in their movements and conversations, not just with each other but with the public in general, neither one wanted to be found out. Not only would it put their lives at risk but also the rest of the network could be discovered if they were to be interrogated.

..........

It had been a few days since Lily had first heard the news about Jack. She spent as much time as she was allowed with him and could see that he was making slow improvements but her experienced eye told her it would be a long recuperation. He no longer had the bandage around his head but his hands were still dressed and his leg was in plaster. The pain was still bad especially in his hands which had been badly burned. He wasn't sleeping as much and could concentrate on conversation for longer periods of time. He still had headaches but they were much improved from the way they had been. There were no concerns about the head injury now. They spent their time saying how much they loved each other and talking about Bobby. Lily had written to Megan and Hugh to tell them what had happened and had a lovely response back to say they would be welcome to visit when Jack was well enough. It would probably be good for Jack to get some fresh country air in him, thought Lily now. That would really cement his recovery.

"I nearly forgot, I had a letter from Ted and Winnie," said Jack. "It's in my locker, why don't you read it."

Lily took the letter from the locker and opened it:

*Dear Jack,*

*We received a letter from dear Lily letting us know what had happened. We were so sorry to hear you had been injured, but glad you will recover eventually. We sincerely hope you feel better soon and then maybe we will meet while you are still recuperating, before you have to go back to base. You probably won't be able to hold this letter because of your poor hands but hope someone will read it to you. Please be assured we are always here for Lily should she need support. She has become like a daughter to us, the daughter we always longed for but never had. We are sure you will pass this letter to her for her to read so she knows we are thinking of you both and long to see her again.*

*Get well soon*
*Ted and Winnie.*

There were tears in Lily's eyes as she read the lovely letter. She felt that at last she had found someone who really cared about her and saw her as a daughter, just as she looked on them as her parents, the parents she never had. "That's a lovely letter," she said at last.

"It is isn't it? They don't know me but seem to have taken me to their heart as well as you," said Jack.

"How are the other men on the ward? Are they friendly?" asked Lily.

"Yeah, there is a great sense of camaraderie here, we've all been injured to varying degrees fighting the enemy. Some have been more injured than I have been. One poor guy at the end of the ward has been blinded. He is struggling to cope with it, poor devil. The guy in the bed opposite lost both his legs in a blast that hit the station he's based at. I got off lightly really, it could've been so much worse. I'll recover and get back to base and fly again." What he didn't say was that some had died of their injuries since he had been there. He didn't want to put that thought in Lily's mind and make her worry, especially as one guy had been doing really well and there was talk of him going home when suddenly he deteriorated and died. It had come as a shock to all of the patients and staff. A timely reminder of how fragile life really was. You couldn't take anything for granted in these uncertain times.

At that moment the doctor came along wanting to check Jack's hands. It was a relief and took his mind off the depressing thoughts of men dying of their injuries. The dressings were taken off and the doctor examined his hands which looked just the same to Jack.

"Well, these look as if they are doing ok," said the doctor in a jovial manner. "How's the pain?"

"Just the same, are they really getting better as they don't look it or feel it?"

"It will take time but yes, they are as I would expect them to be at this stage. How's the leg?"

"That's ok," replied Jack. The leg didn't bother him, it was his hands that were the most troublesome of his injuries.

"Good, good, I'll leave the nurse to put another dressing on your hands and I'll see you tomorrow."

Lily had taken the opportunity to have a good look at the injured hands and formed her own opinions based on her knowledge of nursing.

"What do you think love?" asked Jack when the nurse had dressed the hands and moved away.

"They're doing well," said Lily, truthfully. For indeed they did look good, no sign of infection and some of the rawness had gone out from around the edges of the burns.

"Really?" queried Jack, "They don't feel it."

"Believe me, they are doing well. You'll still be in pain, but they are improving, just as I would expect them to look at this stage after the incident. I'm really pleased with them," she said, sounding more professional than that of his wife.

"If you say so, I'll believe what you say. I never know whether I should believe the staff or not, they might just be trying to jolly me along."

Lily understood what he was saying. Some were like that, wanting to make the patients believe they were doing well even if they weren't, just to keep morale up and prevent the patients slipping into despair. But his injuries really did look good. She was very pleased to see them and form her own judgements based on her experience as a nurse. This had been the first time she had seen the injuries Jack had suffered, having never been here before when the dressings had been changed or when the doctor had come around. She felt relieved now, to see them for herself, she knew Jack would soon be feeling a lot better and in a lot less pain. His hands would be fine. His leg was just a matter of time and that would be fine as well.

"What are you thinking about love," asked Jack.

"I was just thinking about your hands, and how relieved I am to have seen them for myself, they are really doing well and soon I'd expect you to be in less pain. They're healing my darling."

Jack smiled at his wife whom he adored. It was so good to have her by his side again. He had really missed her all those months spent fighting in the air against the Germans. He was just sad that he couldn't give her a cuddle and just hold her in his arms. How he longed to do that but it would have to wait until he was more able.

"Soon you'll be out of here, then we can plan a few days away visiting Bobby. I can't wait for the three of us to be together again even if it can only be for a few short days. A family again just as it should be."

"I know. It'll be a wonderful time together. I can't wait either. It was a really good idea of yours," replied Jack. The thought of the three of them together again, even if it could only be for a short time was what kept him going. It would be so easy to slip into depression with the pain he was enduring and all the suffering on the ward in general, that having something else to think about took his mind off his injuries and life on the ward. Lily had done the right thing when she suggested it.

"As soon as we get some idea of when you will be discharged I'll write to Megan and Hugh and try to arrange something definite," said Lily, pleased that Jack was so enthusiastic about it, although not surprised as he had doted on his young son before the war had split the family up, all of them in different locations across the country. She just hoped this war would end so that they could be together again permanently, but that didn't look like happening anytime soon.

…………..

It was a few weeks later when Jack was up and about on crutches, hobbling about the ward that he was told he would be discharged in the next week or two. His hands had healed nicely and caused no more pain and the dressings had been taken off permanently the week before. The only sign of any injury to his hands were the scars left from the burns. He knew he was lucky to be alive and that the injuries weren't as bad as they could have been. He would be back on the base flying the wonderful spitfires in no time. Although he looked forward to taking an active part in the war again he dreaded having to leave Lily. He had grown used to having her around every day and wanted it to continue, but knew it couldn't with no end to the war in sight.

Lily had also been having similar thoughts going through her head. She was glad that he was being discharged soon but dreaded the time that he would be declared fit for active duty and have to go back to his base. The weeks had flown by and all too soon he would be gone again. If only this war would end but there was no end in sight. The Blitz as it was becoming known as, was still going strong with the dreaded air raid sirens going off still a frequent occurrence at night and

128

sometimes during the day. In spite of this, the spirit of the people hadn't been dampened at all, everyone remained cheerful and helped each other out where necessary. She missed her work at the hospital though and looked forward to being back there soon.

## Chapter Nine

"I'm sorry you're not going to get to meet Ted and Winnie this time," said Lily, "I really wanted you to meet them but as we are going to spend time with Bobby we won't be able to do everything."

"Hopefully I'll get some proper leave sometime and then I can. I'm longing to meet them and I know they are eager to meet me. It would be good for Bobby to meet them to feel he has grandparents," Jack said. His mum had died a year after his marriage to Lily and his dad had died just a few months later. He had never got over losing his wife and Jack and Lily believed he had died of a broken heart having never been able to function on his own. They had been a very close, loving couple. Lily and Jack had just been pleased that they had been around for the wedding, to share their special day. They had loved Lily like a daughter, having been drawn to her serious, sad look.

"I can't wait to see little Bobby again," said Lily, hugging herself with excitement. "Although he isn't so little now according to Hugh and Megan. I just wish we could bring him back home with us. They said they would let Bobby know we were coming. I hope he'll remember us as it has been a long time now. "

"I'm sure he will," said Jack reassuringly, putting an arm around his wife and pulling her close.

Jack had made a full recovery from his injuries and was looking forward to the holiday before having to be back at base in ten days time. Except for a slight limp no one would ever guess that he had been injured doing his duty to his country in this time of war.

Packing done they spent a quiet evening together. For once the siren did not disturb them and they had a nice uninterrupted night's sleep in a comfortable bed instead of the shelter which they both hated with a passion.

Next morning they were up bright and early and looking outside they saw the sun was shining brightly in a nice clear blue sky. It was the perfect day for travelling to Wales. The nice weather filled them both with optimism. They would soon be reunited with their son and would have a wonderful time, they were sure of it. They just had to pop in to see Joan and Arthur before they went. It would be a struggle for Joan to cope with her husband on her own as he was getting worse as time went on. In his mind he was permanently back in the trenches of the Western Front battling the enemy and always trying to pull Joan down with him to keep her safe, stopping her from getting shot at by revealing herself above the trenches. Every time they were meant to go over the top and advance towards the Germans on the other side of no mans land he became very distressed and it took Joan all her time to calm him down. Joan, as a result of this was completely exhausted, always having to reassure Arthur that he was safe and they were not going to be shot at by the enemy. Of course there was the real threat that was posed in the air from the Germans but Arthur seemed completely unaware of this. He was still back enduring the trench warfare of the Great War.

Joan quickly answered the door when Lily and Jack knocked.

"It's going to be a bad day," said Joan, indicating the living room with a nod of her head in that direction, where Arthur was crouching behind a chair which in his mind was the trenches.

As they entered the living room Arthur cried out in panic and tried to hide further, convinced that Lily and Jack were the Germans invading the British trenches. Joan rushed over to him, trying to make soothing sounds to let him know he was safe, he was at home.

Lily and Jack looked at each other, they had no idea how bad it was until they were witnessing it for themselves. They had known from what Joan had been saying recently but had never witnessed it.

"It's all right," Joan said quietly to her husband, reaching out slowly to touch his arm. She had to take it slowly and quietly to avoid spooking Arthur out further. "These are our friends Lily and Jack."

Lily tried approaching, wanting to help her friend, but stopped when Joan with a shake of her head held up her hand to halt her. It seemed when Arthur was like this nothing would be able to convince him that Lily was not the enemy and walking towards him would just cause total panic to break out. Joan didn't know if he would turn violent, convinced he was battling the enemy but she wasn't taking any chances.

Lily and Jack didn't stay long realising their presence was causing too much distress to Arthur. Joan saw them out very apologetically, saying, "I'm so sorry about that. I just don't know what to do for the best anymore. I don't want him to be institutionalised but I'm at my wits end and he's just deteriorating."

"It's hard for you," said Lily sympathetically. "I wouldn't know what to do for the best either. But at the moment you seem to be able to get through to him so that is something. If he were institutionalised he would be disorientated further which would cause more deterioration. I think he's better off where he is for the moment if you can manage him at home."

"Thanks, I think you're probably right and I appreciate your opinion as an onlooker as you're seeing the situation from a different perspective. I can't be objective as you can. It is too personal for me."

"I'll drop round when we get back from Wales and see how he is, we can always talk about things further then." Lily gave Joan a hug. This was a new thing for Lily, she never hugged anyone, always preferring to keep her distance to avoid getting hurt and rejected again. This was just further evidence that Ted and Winnie were good for her.

Jack noticed the hug but said nothing, not wanting to make Lily feel self conscious and withdraw into herself again. He was really seeing the good that Ted and Winnie were for her and couldn't wait to meet them to thank them for helping his darling wife.

..........

"I'm so excited," said Lily, hugging herself with excitement. She couldn't contain how she felt. They were almost there, in a short while she would see her beloved Bobby again. Jack was more contained but he was also looking forward to it. It had been too long and they were looking forward to seeing the changes in their son. They had spent most of the journey talking about him and wondering what he would be like now. They had updates from Megan and Hugh but it wasn't the same as seeing him themselves.

The train slowed down as they approached the station they had been told to get off at. The whistle blew and smoke billowed upwards as the train drew to a halt. It had been a long journey and they couldn't wait to get off and stretch their legs a bit. They were being met by a farmer who would bring his horse and cart to meet them. It had seemed strange to them to be met by a horse and cart instead of a car, but this was the country and there weren't many cars in the small village Megan and Hugh lived, they had explained this in the letter making all the arrangements.

Jack and Lily stood up and stretched, it had been a long time sitting and their muscles felt cramped. Lily took their suitcase and carried it off the train as Jack followed. He still walked with a limp and wasn't quite strong enough to carry the suitcase as well. They both hoped that the fresh country air and undisturbed nights would help to strengthen him further and get him back to normal.

Once off the train they looked around, wondering if their lift had arrived and what he would look like. They stood uncertainly until a man approached them. He had a moustache and beard. He spoke to them with a strong Welsh accent. "Hello, are you Jack and Lily, going to Megan and Hugh?" He spoke with a deep voice and the lilting Welsh accent made him a pleasure to listen too.

"Yes," replied Jack.

"Come on then. I'm Owen, they arranged for me to give you a lift to their house. You must be looking forward to seeing your boy, it's been such a long time. You'll find a difference in him, he's grown since then and he's settled into country life. He visits my farm sometimes at weekends, he loves to see my cows and pigs and help with them. Megan and Hugh have chickens and he loves going out and feeding them and collecting the eggs."

Throwing their suitcase on to the cart he motioned them to get up beside him. Jack needed some help to take the step up because of his bad leg but he got up with help from Owen and Lily.

"You got it bad, did you?" asked Owen.

"Broken leg and burns on my hands," replied Jack shortly. He didn't want to go into details as it might only fuel his nightmares again. They had only just started to wear off a bit, he didn't like thinking of what had happened. He had been haunted by bad dreams ever since he was shot down but they were easing off now and weren't occurring every night.

Owen, realising Jack didn't want to talk about it said no more on the subject and changed topic. "Megan and Hugh are a lovely couple, would do anything for anybody. Everyone in the village respects them and holds them in high regard. If anyone has a problem they can turn to them and they'll help if they can. It's a shame they couldn't have children, they would have been good parents."

"I'm glad Bobby went to such good people," said Lily, speaking for the first time. She had been overawed by this big man with the bushy beard and moustache, brown to match his hair. He had brown eyes as well. He seemed a kindly, cheerful man but Lily was quiet around strangers, very serious and sad.

Owen had noticed that and wondered about her. Surely it couldn't just be her husband's injuries that caused her to look so serious and sad. Bobby being evacuated must have been a huge wrench for her especially as Bobby was so young, but she would have known he had gone to a good home. Yes, that might account for the sad look on her face but why did she look so serious. Lily was having an effect on him as she seemed to on most people. Maybe she would lighten up when she was reunited with her little boy but somehow he doubted it. The serious, sad look went too deep he felt.

It wasn't long before they drew to a halt outside a lovely looking cottage. There were different coloured flowers outside, reds, yellows and pinks all mixed together. Lily couldn't take her eyes off them. It gave the cottage a homely, pleasant feel to it. She hadn't known what to expect but this was lovely. There weren't many gardens with flowers in London so this was all new to her and she loved it. The cottage seemed small but welcoming. It looked well maintained and she couldn't wait to see inside.

She took Jack's hand and they stood together staring at this lovely sight before them.

"Come on then," said Owen, "are you going inside or not?" he asked, amused. He wasn't to know they were too busy drinking in the sight before them, having never seen anything like this before. It was so quiet and peaceful and the air smelled so fresh and clean. No dirty, smoky smell that they were used to. They looked at each other and smiled, there was no need for words, they knew what the other was thinking. Yes, this would be a good place to spend the next few days and Jack hoped it would end his nightmares forever. A wonderful place to finish recuperating.

Megan and Hugh had been looking out for them and now Megan turned to Bobby and said, "Your mummy and daddy are here darling, shall we open the door for them to come in. They must be dying to see you."

Megan, accompanied by Hugh and Bobby went to the front door and opened it. "Hello," she cried. "You must be Jack and Lily, I'm Megan and this is Hugh and of course you know Bobby."

"Bobby," cried Lily, letting go of Jack and rushing through the wrought iron gate and up the path. She stopped as she reached Bobby and crouched down.

"Hello Bobby," she said quietly, for Bobby was hiding behind Megan just peeping out from behind her legs every now and again.

"Mummy?" he queried.

"That's right darling. Daddy is with me as well. Daddy hasn't been very well so we thought we would spend a few days here before he has to go back to flying aeroplanes."

"Mummy and Daddy," he said, slowly coming out from behind Megan. "I've been drawing pictures for you, have you been seeing them."

"Yes, darling, we've seen them, they are beautiful just like you."

"Mummy and Daddy," he cried, finally moving away from Megan and running into Lily's waiting arms. "I love you and I've missed you so much."

"So have we darling."

"Hey, what about me?" asked Jack. "Don't I get a hug?"

"Daddy," said Bobby, leaving Lily and went into Jack's waiting arms.

"Sorry I can't pick you up and swing you round like I used to but I've got a bad leg."

"Your leg not well," said Bobby.

"No darling. I got hurt in my plane." Jack said. Not saying too much as he didn't want his small son to know anything of the violence that was taking place in the world. It was bad enough that they were separated from their son but he was safe here away from the dangers of the frequent bombing raids.

"Come on, why don't we go inside," said Megan, leading the way back into the little cottage.

Lily looked around and thought how well cared for it was, just like the outside.  The table had a vase of flowers on presumably taken from the garden. They created a nice fresh smell in the room. On the mantelpiece stood photographs, one of which was of her, Jack and Bobby. She was pleased to see it there, it meant Bobby would see it all the time and know who his parents were. There were very comfortable chairs in the room that looked well stuffed and soft, as if one would sink into them when sitting down, like a nice feather pillow.

"Sit down," said Hugh, "We've put the kettle on so a cup of tea will be ready in a jiffy. You must be gasping for a cuppa."

"We are rather," said Jack, speaking for both of them, seeing Lily was still gazing around the room in awe.

They sat down and as expected sank into the lovely soft chairs.

"I love these chairs, so soft," said Lily. "I feel as if I'm sinking into a pile of feathers."

"I agree," said Jack, "So much better than the hard seats in the train."

"Thank you," said Hugh. "They're so different from the chairs that seem to be fashion at the moment but we prefer them for the comfort they provide."

"I've never come across any like these before," said Lily.

"You won't find many people have them in their houses at the moment. I happen to know the designer so he made them specially for us. He hopes they will sell and become popular at some point."

At that moment Megan brought the tray with the tea through. She poured it out, handing a cup to both Jack and Lily. She handed a cup of orange to Bobby. "Here you are, you must be gasping."

There was silence as they all drank their tea. Jack and Lily were tired and couldn't make conversation. Lily was doing all she could to keep from yawning. They had been up early and then the long train journey had tired her out completely. These soft chairs had her nearly falling asleep.

Megan noticed this, but kept quiet until they had finished their tea, then she said, "Why don't I take you upstairs and you can see your room. You can unpack and have a lie down, you must be tired after the long journey."

"We are rather," said Jack, stifling a yawn.

They went upstairs and found the room just as comfortable and welcoming as downstairs had been. They didn't even bother unpacking they just collapsed on the bed and fell asleep.

"When are mummy and daddy coming down?" asked Bobby.

"They'll be down later dear. They're tired because they have come a long way and want to sleep for a bit. So be a good boy and play quietly."

Bobby nodded and settled down with cars that he had been playing with before his parents had arrived. Megan looked at him fondly, he was a good boy, rarely disobeying. Hugh got on the floor with him and they pushed the car back and forwards to each other. Bobby loved this game and could go on like this for hours. It didn't take much to amuse the little boy. While Hugh kept Bobby occupied Megan went to the small kitchen to prepare the tea as she was sure Lily and Jack would be hungry after having a rest and as for Bobby he was always wanting food.

Jack and Lily fell asleep instantly, so tired from the long journey. Lily awoke a couple of hours later and nudged Jack. "Come on, wake up, Bobby will be wondering where we are, and it's a bit rude of us to sleep when we've just arrived."

Jack mumbled something but didn't stir.

Lily shook him again, "Jack, we really should get up and go downstairs."

Jack jolted awake, "What? Where are we?" he asked, looking around confused at first, then remembering got up quickly. They both went downstairs.

"So sorry we were so long, we fell asleep," said Jack apologetically.

"Don't worry about it," said Megan warmly, "You were tired and it was a long journey. Journeys can be so tiring. Now you're awake you must be hungry, I've got a nice shepherds pie for you and in the morning you can have a nice fresh egg, none of that powdered rubbish for us. Living in the country has its advantages and being good friends with Owen helps, he's always happy to help out when it comes to food."

They sat down at the table, Bobby in between Jack and Lily, talking nineteen to the dozen.

"Is he always like this?" asked Jack, with a laugh at his small son's chatter.

"Yes, he never stops, from morning until night," responded Hugh. "He is very bright and picks things up quickly. He's doing well at school and has loads of friends."

"You'll have to show us what you're learning at school son," said Jack, ruffling his son's hair fondly.

"1x2=2,
2x2=4,
3x2=6,
4x2=8…"

"That's very good Bobby," said Lily, cutting him off before he could recite the whole of the two times table.

Lily and Jack looked at each other over Bobby's head and smiled. It was so good to be reunited with him again and hearing what he had been learning in school. He was obviously very bright and learning things quickly.

"He's very good in maths, that is his best subject," said Hugh.

"This is nice," said Jack, savouring every mouthful. "I haven't had anything this nice for ages. RAF food isn't always the best and of course with rationing we have to be so careful with food,"

"And there's so little in the shops these days," added Lily.

She and Joan often had these conversations about rationing which everyone was having, just standing in queues in the shops confirmed this. So many things were unavailable these days, thanks to Hitler.

"Blinking Hitler has a lot to answer for," said Lily, smiling to herself as she found herself using one of Winnie's favourite words.

Jack looked at her in surprise, he had never heard her use that word before, but he didn't know Ted and Winnie except through letters and that word hadn't been used yet. Megan frowned, she believed in using correct English at all times. There was no need for adding such words into common usage and certainly not in front of children who were so impressionable, copying what they hear others say.

"Sorry," said Lily, seeing Megan's frown. "I'm so used to hearing that word from a friend it just slips out sometimes."

Jack guessed at which friend this was. It could only be from her new friends Ted and Winnie and somehow coming from them it seemed right. He had never heard Joan use that word and Lily didn't have many friends.

Unfortunately Bobby had been listening intently to the adults talking and now decided it would be fun to use this new word. "Blinking, blinking, blinking," he said in a sing song voice.

"No Bobby," said Lily, feeling ashamed for using it in front of the small boy. "It isn't right to use that word. I'm sorry I shouldn't have used it and neither should you," she admonished.

"Ok, mummy," said Bobby casually. He had only been copying Lily and had no idea what it meant or why she used it. He had never heard it before and it had captured his interest.

"Bobby it's time for you to get ready for bed now," said Megan, thinking it best to change the subject. Bobby was looking tired and they were eating later than usual because they had been waiting for Jack and Lily to come down. "Maybe Mummy will go up with you and help you tonight and give you a goodnight kiss."

"I'll help as well," said Jack. "I have missed this bedtime routine and would love to spend time with Bobby."

"Yes," cried Bobby. That sounded good to him. This was going to be fun spending time with his parents. He didn't know how long they were there for but if they were going to be there in the morning he would show them the chickens and how he collected the eggs. He was proud of his morning job and wanted to please his parents.

The three of them went upstairs. Bobby was soon ready for bed and tucked in. Jack and Lily sat on either side of the bed with their son, wanting to soak up every minute they spent with him. He had grown so much and they wanted memories to take away with them when these few days were over.

Downstairs again they sat with Megan and Hugh.

Lily said, "Thank you for looking after Bobby so well for us. He's obviously happy here and he's safe." Lily's face clouded as she thought of the state London was in, the disturbed nights, the rubble and smoke in the air. Not healthy or safe for anyone and certainly not for a small child.

"Is it bad?" queried Hugh.

"It's not nice," responded Lily. "The air raids day and night, the bombs. So many houses and lives destroyed. So much devastation, I don't know when it's all going to end."

"You two must be tired, why don't you have an early night," said Megan stepping in, seeing the distressed look on Lily's face at the thought of what they had left behind in London. This was supposed to be a break away from it all and she wanted them to go back refreshed in body and mind.

Jack and Lily didn't stir all night, worn out from the journey and from nights broken by bombing. They were woken up early by the sound of cock a doodle doo from a cockerel. They got up, going to check on Bobby. They found him awake and playing with a car again. Giving him a hug they asked what he does first.

"I get up and Megan helps me dress then I collect the eggs for the day," the little boy said eagerly.

Lily enjoyed helping her son to dress although he could manage most of it himself. He led the way downstairs and outside to the chickens.

"Hello," he said to the chickens, naming them all. They all looked alike to Lily but Bobby seemed to know the difference which was the important thing. Turning to his parents he said, "This one's Tim, he's my favourite, Hugh let me name him,"

Watching him carefully, Lily could see he knew exactly what he was doing as he quickly collected the eggs awaiting him. He carefully placed them in the basket he was holding and took them inside to Megan who was in the kitchen waiting for them.

"We used to get a few broken eggs at first," said Megan with a laugh, thinking back to the first few days Bobby collected the eggs. "But he has learned now and none get broken. He can be so gentle for his age, he's really a pleasure to have around. You should be so proud of him."

"We are," said Jack, showing it by giving a fond look towards his son.

They enjoyed scrambled egg for breakfast, then as it was a Sunday Megan said they would be going to church in the village. Jack and Lily weren't churchgoers but didn't want to alter the routine of the house so they agreed to go with them.

Once the service was over Megan and Hugh introduced them to friends. Lily being on the quiet side felt a bit uncomfortable with this but was able to murmur hello. Bobby raced around with other small boys his age. Megan commented that they were his friends from school.

After lunch they sat quietly watching Bobby playing with his toys. They weren't surprised to see him playing with the same car as yesterday. It seemed to be a favourite of his. This time it was Jack who pushed the car backwards and forwards across the floor.

The next day Megan took Bobby to school accompanied by Jack and Lily. Bobby was reluctant, wanting to stay home with his parents, but they insisted he had to go to school as normal, promising to collect him at the end of the day. They walked along swinging Bobby between them. They looked at each other, both feeling the same contentment. Being together after being apart for so long was too wonderful to put into words.

They walked slowly back to the cottage wanting to have a good look around the small village. It looked just as picturesque as Megan and Hugh's cottage looked. All had flowers growing in small gardens. So many different colours, each a contrast to the others. To look at, it looked as if no war was going on, it was completely untouched by any signs of war. There were signs of chickens and some goats. Megan suggested they have a walk to Owen's farm so they could have a look around there, having never been near a farm before.

Owen was more than happy to show them around the farm. The cows were out in the fields now having been milked earlier. They also saw pigs and goats. He invited them to visit during milking time so they could see the process take place. Jack and Lily readily agreed, they were keen to see everything and were just like small children in their eagerness to look around.

Back at the cottage Lily said, "You would never know there's a war on, this place is like being on a different planet, everyone going about their business and the flowers growing are so beautiful. I wish I could stay here forever. It's nice to know Hitler hasn't completely destroyed the country, although he's had a good try. This is such a good place for Bobby to be. I'm glad he is shut away from the mayhem and chaos the world is in at the moment."

"You're right," said Megan, "We only find out what is happening on the wireless when we listen to the news. We have remained untouched here for which we're very grateful."

"I wish we didn't have to go back to the real world in a few days, to stay here shut away would be wonderful," said Jack.

"But we need people like you to fight for us to keep us free from Nazism," said Hugh.

"I suppose so, but sometimes the real world seems too scary a place to be in. To be constantly on edge, not knowing what will happen next is very trying and exhausting sometimes," replied Jack.

"Also there is the nightly battle going on overhead. Nights spent in the shelters, not knowing what we'll find the next morning. Not knowing if we'll still have a house left or if people we know have been killed or injured," said Lily.

"It must be a nightmare," agreed Megan. "Why don't we change the subject, you haven't come here to talk about the war. You're supposed to be having a complete rest from it all. A break from the fighting and bombing, of being always on edge not knowing what will happen next."

They spent a pleasant time until it was time to collect Bobby from school. They talked about him a lot and how he was growing so quickly. He was so happy with Megan and Hugh and Jack and

Lily could see this for which they were very grateful. He was doing well at school, was obviously very bright. He seemed to be especially good at maths and worked hard at it.

When Bobby came out of school he saw his parents and ran to them shouting delightedly, "Mummy! Daddy! You came!"

"Whoa, you'll knock me over," said Jack laughing, for Bobby had flung himself into Jack's waiting arms.

Jack held Bobby away from him, soaking up the happy little face before him. This is how he wanted to remember Bobby when he was back at base, flying the Spitfires to defend his country. He was pleased to see Bobby so happy.

"Bye," called another boy to Bobby.

"Bye Dave," called Bobby back.

"Is he one of your friends?" asked Lily.

"Yes, he was 'vacued, the same as me," said Bobby unable to say the word evacuated.

Jack and Lily smiled at each other over Bobby's head. Bobby obviously had an understanding of what had happened, but they didn't know if he understood why he had to be evacuated. He was still so young, they wanted him to keep his innocence for a few years yet.

"We play flying games together in the playground," said Bobby.

"What is that?" asked Jack.

"We pretend to be planes flying and bombing each other, just like the planes we see flying in the sky."

Jack and Lily looked at each other, not as innocent as they had hoped. But did he really understand what was happening in the world? They hoped it was a fun game to him with no understanding of the reality that was taking place.

That evening when Bobby was in bed Lily asked Megan and Hugh about it.

"It's impossible to hide the reality from him completely. He hears things from the others at school especially the older children. I don't think he really understands what is happening or that people are being killed. It's just a game to him," said Hugh.

"Good," said Jack. "We don't want to think his childhood is being marred by what is happening in the world."

"You don't have to worry too much, he's very much a five year old boy," said Megan, trying to reassure the anxious parents.

..........

The days passed quickly and soon Jack and Lily were thinking of leaving. Jack had really benefited from the days away, he looked much fitter than when he had arrived. Lily, too, had lost the pale, listlessness that had been there. The shadows had gone from under her eyes. Unbroken sleep had really helped them both.

"Well we're all packed and ready," said Lily on their final evening. They would be leaving the next day after taking Bobby to school. Owen had agreed to take them to the station.

"We've had a really good time and I feel more relaxed now," said Jack.

"You look so much better than when you arrived, you both do."

"We feel it," said Lily. "There have been air raids every day and night which makes it difficult to sleep or rest at all. I really needed a break from it all. The shelters are not exactly designed for comfort. They're monstrosities."

"We can't even begin to imagine what you must have been through, it sounds awful, absolutely awful," said Hugh. "I just hope things will have improved when you get back."

"Maybe," said Lily, unconvinced, she couldn't even imagine a time without air raids, they had been going on so long. She dreaded what they would find when they got back to London.

## Chapter Ten

Lily was back at work at the hospital and Jack had been back at the base for ten days now. Lily worried constantly about him, worried he would get hurt or worse next time. She had quickly got back in the swing of things completely refreshed from the short holiday in Wales.

She had been able to spend a day with Winnie and Ted since being back, they had been pleased to see how well she was doing and how happy she was. They had become very fond of Lily in the short time they had known her. They were as funny as ever and she had received the handbag treatment although she was unsure why. It had been good to spend time with them after seeing Jack off, it had taken her mind off the goodbye. She enjoyed telling them about the wonderful time in Wales spent with Bobby. She didn't know what she had done to deserve such good friends in her life but she was very grateful for them.

…………

Jack had got back to base enthusiastic, ready to get up in his beloved Spitfire and continue fighting the Luftwaffe. Everyone had welcomed him back, glad to see him in one piece. He had enjoyed the camaraderie of the mess once again. There were new faces and other old faces missing which saddened him. Some of the missing faces were now trapped in prisoner of war camps but others hadn't been so lucky and had died. Not so lucky? He thought. Maybe those who hadn't survived were the lucky ones, no one knew how prisoners were being treated by the enemy.

It had been good to catch up on all the news and now he was back flying again. He quickly remembered what he loved about this fighter plane. He loved hearing the whirring of the engine starting up and the feeling of power he felt when it took off into the air, apparently without effort. Nothing could compare to the exhilaration he felt, he just wished he were flying under different circumstances so that he could be relaxed up there instead of constantly alert, on the look out for the enemy.

When he landed he had a grin on his face, it had felt so good, a reminder of what he had missed. It wasn't just the flying it was the camaraderie with the others on the base. They were like a family all joined together in a common cause.

He went to the mess still grinning from ear to ear.

"You obviously enjoyed that," said James coming up to him and slapping him on the back. "It's good to have you with us again. There is nothing like that feeling of being free up in the air is there." It was a rhetorical question so Jack didn't answer, anyway there was nothing to say really. His face said it all.

………

Lily was having a very much needed weekend off. It had been two months now since they had returned from Wales visiting Bobby. She intended popping into see Joan and Arthur before going to Ted and Winnie's. Lily stepped outside and shivered, pulling her coat firmly around her, it was a very cold February day. She was glad to get into the warmth of Joan's house. There was a roaring fire in the grate and Lily went straight towards it, holding her hands out to warm them up.

"Brr, it's freezing out there," commented Lily. "I think we will have snow if it stays cold like this."

"I don't envy you, being out in it. I have no intention of going anywhere."

Arthur was sitting on the floor in the corner rocking and mumbling to himself. He was permanently in a world of his own now, nothing Joan or Lily said could reach him. In his mind he just wasn't there, he was some place else, experiencing all sorts of horrors.

"No change then," said Lily, "He seems too far gone now."

"Yes he is, I'm feeding him now or he does nothing just sits staring into space, mumbling. He opens his mouth but I could be giving him anything, he takes no notice at all. I've given up coaxing him to try to feed himself, he doesn't seem to hear me." Joan shook her head sadly. "It's so heartbreaking. If only Hitler hadn't come along Arthur would've been the same as he was when he came home a broken man, now he just isn't there. I've lost my husband, he may be there in body but it's just the shell, the man I love has gone forever."

Lily put her arm around her friend but said nothing. What could she say, there were no words that could bring comfort where there was no comfort or hope. She wished she could do more but there was nothing. Joan had lost her daughter and her husband, thanks to Hitler. He had a lot to answer for in her opinion. Joan's situation was just another tragedy of this war.

Joan gave herself a shake and said, "Anyway have you got time to stay for a cuppa,"

"Yes, I think so," said Lily.

Lily sat at the table while Joan went off to make the tea, if that's what you could call the pale liquid. Joan came back carrying a tray with a pot of tea with a knitted tea cosy and cups.

"Sorry, I've no biscuits or sugar," she said.

"That's ok, it doesn't matter, we're all in the same boat."

"I know, but I still find myself apologising and somehow trying to justify it."

Lily sipped the hot, tasteless liquid and sighed. "What I wouldn't give for a proper cuppa and a biscuit."

"Dream on," said Joan. "I can't even remember what that would taste like."

"And what about oranges and bananas," said Lily.

"Don't torture me, that would be heaven, but we can only dream and hope this war will be over soon."

"No sign of that happening though," said Lily. "We just have to make the best of things as they are at the moment."

There was more chit chat between the two friends before Lily said, "Well I better get off if I'm to get to Ted and Winnie's. These days you never know how long a ten minute journey is going to take." She stood up and put her coat on saying, "Thanks for the tea."

"No problem, it took my mind off Arthur for a bit. He won't even go to bed now, just stays there as if on guard, but at the same time hiding."

Lily got on the bus and sat huddled in the seat trying to get warm. It really was very cold. As she sat looking out of the window she saw a few flakes of snow starting to fall. Well, it wasn't a surprise really, it had been on the cards considering how bitterly cold it was. She had better make sure she didn't stay too long with that funny couple or she might have problems getting home if the snow continued. The journey was very slow going because of the weather and the conditions caused by the bombing.

Lily saw a few people walking along the road, shoulders slumped as if in despair. It wasn't surprising, life really had become very grim and there was no end in sight. Bombed buildings, rubble everywhere. There was no sign of anything changing which was so depressing, but somehow people just carried on. Amongst all the complaints about the hardships this war had caused, there was still plenty of humour, showing that the spirit of the British people had not been broken and never would be. They were only a small island but it had plenty of fight left in it yet.

Lily thought of the couple she was on her way to see, yes they just proved the people had not given in and never would. One would always find a reason to laugh and Ted and Winnie were proof of that. She smiled at the thought. She anticipated a good time with this couple who were like parents to her.

She got up ready to get off. She felt stiff having been sat in the cold for some time. She couldn't wait to get to her destination, she was sure of a warm welcome and the heat of a fire.

She fell into Winnie's arms when she arrived. It was so nice to be there receiving the hugs she couldn't remember in her childhood.

"Come on in you daft 'apporth, you are letting the cold in standing on the doorstep like that."

"Sorry," said Lily looking ashamed.

"Don't worry about it, I'm only joking, although it's very cold and starting to snow."

Lily stood back, letting go of Winnie and they went inside, Winnie shutting the door behind them

Ted was stood waiting for the hug he knew was coming and sure enough Lily went straight into his arms, not caring about the consequences which were quickly coming.

"Hey you, don't snatch my man from me," said Winnie lifting her handbag and knocking Lily over the head with it. The three of them laughed for it was only in fun. "Come and sit down and tell us how you've been."

Lily sat down between her two friends, having taken her coat off. She sighed and told them about her visit to Joan and Arthur. The smiles and laughter stopped at talk of the tragic situation.

Winnie poured the tea and handed Lily the cup. Lily cradled the cup in her hands wanting to warm her freezing palms and fingers.

"Just what we need on a freezing day like this," commented Winnie, "It will soon warm you up."

Lily sipped the hot water, as that was what tea was like these days, just insipid liquid.

"That'll warm you up at least. It won't do much else though," commented Ted.

"We have no choice but to put up with these inconveniences," returned Lily. "At least what we go through isn't as much as what our men go through every day in the forces."

"Have you heard anything from Jack?" queried Winnie.

Lily's face looked despairing at the question and she swallowed before answering, "No, nothing since he went back."

"I'm sure he'll be fine," said Winnie, patting Lily's arm, wanting to be of some comfort to the girl she had become so fond of and saw as the daughter she never had.

"I know. He'll be busy. I'd have been notified if anything had happened. They were quick to let me know when he was injured."

Lily sounded quite positive which was unusual for her, thought Winnie, looking over at Ted and catching his eye raised her eyebrows. He understood the unspoken message and gave a small nod.

"I've had pictures from Bobby though which I have brought with me if you want to see them."

"Of course we do," said Winnie.

Lily got the pictures out of her bag and a brief note from her son. Ted and Winnie were enthusiastic in their praise of Lily's son, especially at the note in very childish handwriting. This was the first note Lily had received written by her son so was really proud of it. When the oohs and aahs were over Lily put them carefully back in her bag.

"Anyway, how've you been, since I last saw you?" asked Lily, realising they had only talked about her since she had arrived.

"We're fine, not liking this blinking cold weather though. The chill gets right into our bones so we feel a bit stiff at times. Never mind though, we mustn't complain, there are worse things to endure in these difficult days," said Winnie.

"At least that is one thing we can't blame Hitler for, the weather," said Lily.

"That's about the only thing we can't blame him for," said Ted, putting his cup down with a grimace. He continued, "I really miss a decent cup of tea and a biscuit."

Winnie was trying to think of something to say that would lift the mood that had become too sombre for her liking.

"At least you're not blaming me for the tea," she said, grinning to herself, she knew which direction she wanted this to go.

Ted, picking up the cue said, "Well, I suppose it is your fault for putting less tea in the teapot."

"Oh yeah, and where do you think I am going to get the blinking tea from? You would soon complain if I ran out of tea and couldn't get anymore," she retorted, starting to enjoy herself now.

"You should just go to the shops and buy some more," Ted quickly came out with the answer. He glanced at Lily and saw her lips quivering. Good, he thought, she was listening avidly to their conversation and forgetting about her family.

"And where do you expect me to buy some more when there isn't any in the shops and I have run out of coupons." Winnie too, had noticed the look on Lily's face and was satisfied. She wasn't finished yet though.

"Well you should insist on keeping some especially for you," responded Ted.

"Oh yeah, and they're really going to break rules just so you can have a blinking cup of tea, not forgetting the favouritism that would show." Winnie's eyes were flashing dangerously and the look on her face spelled trouble.

Lily was enjoying herself now, this was the sort of exchange she came to expect from this couple and she knew where it would end. She noticed Winnie gripping her handbag and knew it would come soon.

Ted also noticed and was ready to duck at any moment. However he was too late and the handbag hit him over the head. Lily burst out laughing, exactly the response Ted and Winnie wanted.

"You'll kill me one of these days," said Lily through the laughter. Tears were pouring down her cheeks, but tears of hilarity not of sadness. She was almost doubled up with the mirth that consumed her. Ted and Winnie watched, satisfied with the response they had got to their piece of nonsense.

Unfortunately when she started laughing Lily had been holding her cup so the hot liquid slopped all over her dress.

"Now look at you, what a mess you've made of that lovely dress," said Winnie, with mock severity. In reality she didn't care as long as Lily was happy, that was the main thing.

"Sorry," said Lily, trying to look contrite but failing because the laughter was still there.

Winnie stood up and went to the kitchen to get a cloth and came back to find Lily trying to get control of herself again. It wouldn't be Winnie though if she didn't react so she grabbed her handbag and before Lily realised what was happening received the blow to the head. This time it was Ted and Winnie's turn to laugh as they saw a rather bemused look on Lily's face.

Lily often wondered what the neighbours would think when hearing all the laughter coming through the thin walls, but she assumed they were used to this pair of jokers. Lily was starting to enjoy herself and thoughts of Jack and Bobby vanished for the time being to the back of her mind. She would think of them later as they were never far from her thoughts, but for now, at least, she had some light relief.

"I wasn't expecting that," said Lily grinning.

"Why not? You know what she's like by now," said Ted.

"I suppose I should've been ready for it, but it was the last thing on my mind."

"Good, I like to take people by surprise," said Winnie, happily. She liked nothing better than making people happy, she loved hearing their merriment. It gave her pleasure, especially when it was Lily as she needed a lot of laughter in her life to make up for the past. Lily was changing though, Winnie realised and was pleased to see it. Lily had been so serious and sad when they first met but that look was starting to vanish now as she responded to their antics. Winnie knew this wouldn't change overnight but they were certainly moving in the right direction.

What Ted and Winnie kept to themselves was the letter they received from Jack before he went back to base to say how pleased he was at the change that he could see in Lily. She was no longer as withdrawn or as serious looking as she had been. She was also much more affectionate, much more tactile in her relationship with him. This he had said was due to them.

"At least we're having a break from air raids for now," said Ted.

"Tell me about it," said Lily, "Transport is still very slow though and so much damage has been done."

. . . . . . . . . . . .

Lily had spent a happy couple of hours with her friends, but now was the time to leave if she wanted to get back before the blackout. She wasn't entirely happy at having to leave this warm house and go back into the cold. She put her coat  and gloves on, preparing to leave. Ted and Winnie were sorry to see her go as they loved spending time with her.

"We'll see you soon then?" asked Ted.

"Definitely," responded Lily. "You don't think you can get rid of me that easily do you."

"Hope not," said Winnie. "We love having you around bringing some youth into the house and into our lives."

Lily opened the door and turned to give Ted and Winnie one last hug before going out into the cold and snow.  There was a blanket of white outside now.

"Are you sure it is a good idea to go back in that? You're welcome to stay here you know," said Ted, worried she would find it too difficult to get home again.

"No, I'll be fine, I'm sure everything will be ok, it's not that bad yet so the buses should be running still."

"Well if you're sure. If you find yourself stranded make sure you come back here. You're more than welcome to spend the night," said Winnie.

Ted and Winnie stood at the door watching her make her slow way up the street towards the bus stop. They looked at each other worrying about Lily. They were unhappy to see her leave in this bad weather but she had been adamant.

Lily's journey home was very slow because of the weather. The snow continued to come down in big flakes. It was nice to look at but made travelling difficult. Finally she succeeded in getting home. It was nearly time for the blackout.

As she passed Joan's house she thought she heard a scream. She hurried up their path and knocked on the door. There was no answer which worried Lily further. What was happening in there? She couldn't look in the windows because the blackout curtains were already closed to keep the light from showing. She tried knocking again but still no answer. She called through the letter box but heard nothing. Looking under the mat that was outside the front door she found a spare key and let herself in, calling out as she did so, not wanting to surprise them and cause panic. She was met with Arthur standing holding Joan lightly around her throat. Not wanting to frighten Arthur and risk harm coming to Joan she crept in slowly and quietly.

"Arthur look at me," she said quietly, "Everything is ok, it's Joan you have got there. Release her. She's not going to hurt you, you are safe now."

"The enemy, a hun, my prisoner," responded Arthur with an authoritative tone in his voice. "Don't come any closer, you're a traitor, I need to shoot you."

"If you want to shoot me you need to let your prisoner go," said Lily responding in the language Arthur had used.

Arthur loosened his grip momentarily which enabled Joan to wriggle her way out. She rushed to Lily who took her in her arms.

"I'm so glad you came, I was so frightened, I don't know what got into him. He suddenly decided I was the enemy and grabbed me, pulling me into his grasp and got my throat. I really thought he was going to kill me this time," said Joan the words coming out in a rush.

"Slow down and tell me exactly what happened, you're safe now," said Lily calmly, although she felt anything but calm. She had been shaken up by the sight she had walked in on.

"I don't know really, I had just come in to give Arthur a cup of tea when he suddenly grabbed me and pulled me to him, with his arm around my throat, telling me I was his prisoner. I couldn't persuade him that he is at home and I'm his wife. I really thought he was going to kill me. I was so scared. I don't know what would have

happened if you hadn't come in at that moment."
Joan gave way to tears of relief, now that she was
safe.

"This can't go on, you know that don't you,"
said Lily. Joan nodded in response.

"He is getting worse, and now he is
becoming a danger to you. We have to do
something before he deteriorates further. I am
unhappy about leaving you here with him."

"I know," said Joan unhappily. "I can't
ignore this any longer. He is getting worse all the
time now."

"I need to get the doctor to come out, but he
will only recommend Arthur goes into an
institution," said Lily.

Joan nodded. She wasn't happy but knew
there was no other option now. She was not
qualified to deal with Arthur any longer.

"Will you be all right here while I fetch the
doctor?" asked Lily, afraid to leave her friend, but
needing to go for help.

Joan nodded. "I'll wait in the kitchen. I
should be ok there, Arthur never leaves this room
anymore."

"I won't be long," said Lily, as she rushed
off.

Lily was true to her word and came back
with the doctor half an hour later. She had waited
for the doctor as he was out on an emergency call.
On hearing what Lily had to say he was happy to
turn back and head off again.

Lily let themselves in when they arrived and Lily showed him through to the kitchen where Joan was waiting.

Joan showed him through to Arthur who was crouching behind the chair again.

"Hello Arthur," said the doctor in a calm voice. Arthur ignored the doctor and continued muttering to himself.

Suddenly Arthur jumped up knocking the chair over in his haste and rushed across the room, nearly knocking the doctor over.

"He thinks the call has come for them to go over the top and advance on the enemy trenches," explained Joan who was so used to her husband and was able to interpret his actions. "This is the first time he has gone at me like that, mistaking me for the enemy."

"You should've called me sooner," admonished the doctor.

"I know, but I really thought I could manage on my own. He hasn't shown any sort of violence until now, but he has been getting worse."

"It's going to be all right, but the situation can't be allowed to continue like this. I'm going to give him an injection of a sedative to calm him initially until I can sort something out. I am recommending he goes into an institution where they're  best placed to look after him and will understand his needs. I don't believe he'll ever recover as he's been slowly deteriorating."

Lily put her arm around Joan who was weeping now. "You know it's the right thing to do. You can't look after him anymore. You've done your best but now it's time to let the professionals take over."

"I know," said Joan, "I still feel I am letting him down though. I'm his wife in sickness and in health. It's my job to look after him."

"Not any longer," said the doctor. "He is very ill and needs specialist care. I can see you have done your best under very difficult circumstances though and I commend you for that, but now you need to let the professionals take over."

Joan nodded and sighed heavily. She hated giving in. She was not someone who quits at the slightest trouble.

It was the next morning that an ambulance arrived to take Arthur. He was still drowsy from the injection the doctor had given him the previous day so didn't try to fight them. Joan was allowed to go with him but shook her head, she couldn't bear to go with him, she would visit him of course, but couldn't be part of having him committed. Lily sighed as she watched the ambulance taking Arthur away. The situation was so sad. She couldn't help thinking of her mother, she was just as much a casualty of war as Arthur. It was only now she was appreciating what it must have been like for her mother and started to feel an ounce of pity for her. War destroyed people in so many ways, it didn't have to be just those who fought either, it was those left behind as well. Lily went over to Joan and put an arm around her. As the ambulance moved out of sight, Joan turned to Lily and fell into her arms sobbing as if her heart would break, as indeed it was. Lily held her close, not knowing what to say, as indeed there were no words of comfort to offer on this occasion. All she could do was be there for her friend.

"You know it's for the best, and you can always visit," said Lily at last, trying to be of some comfort to her friend.

"I suppose so, he was getting too difficult for me to deal with," Joan admitted. "But I feel I've failed by letting him go like that."

"You haven't failed, you did your best in difficult circumstances, there was nothing more you could have done. He was becoming violent towards you, who knows what would have happened if I hadn't come along. He is unlikely to realise you have sent him away as you weren't there anyway in his mind."

"I know what you are saying is true but it doesn't change how I feel."

Lily didn't know how to respond to her friend and just stood holding Joan with a heavy heart. It was just a very sad situation.

………

It was a few weeks later when Lily next saw Ted and Winnie. She told them what had happened and how useless she felt when trying to comfort Joan.

"You weren't useless, you were there and that's what mattered. Joan would've felt your comfort just by being present," said Winnie. "How is she now?"

"She's slowly coming to terms with it," answered Lily. "She's visited a few times but always comes away depressed. Arthur doesn't recognise her. At least there's been no more violence from him according to the staff. You know, I hate to say this but it would almost have been better if he had died in the war instead of the life he lives now. It's not much of a life. The trench warfare is still going on unrelenting in his mind."

Ted nodded, understanding where Lily was coming from. "I can see your point," he said. "She's mourning the loss of the husband she knew and it is ongoing because he's still alive, but not present. If he'd been killed she could have mourned once and for all, but as things stand she can't move on with her life as she's still caught up with him, if you know what I'm trying to say."

Lily nodded. Ted was only saying what she had been thinking. She was glad to have Ted and Winnie to talk to about it as she felt she was being dragged down by it all. Joan was still really struggling and leaning on Lily so much.

"I just don't know what I can do or say to Joan and it isn't long since she lost her daughter," she said, feeling very sad.

"I don't think there's anything you can do love," said Winnie, patting Lily's arm. "You can only be there for her. She'll come to terms with it in her own time. She has to mourn the loss of her husband and also accept that he will never get better and that he's in the best place. She doesn't have anything to feel guilty about but she won't see it like that."

Lily sighed, "It's just so hard. She visits him and then that stirs it all up again in her mind and she starts feeling guilty about not being able to look after him, it's also a reminder that he'll never get any better."

The three of them sat in silence, there was nothing that could be said. Lily was supporting her friend through all these emotions, but that is all she could do and she felt helpless.

"I have visited Arthur with her and it was so very sad to see. He was just sat in the corner rocking and mumbling to himself. He was sat on the floor with a chair in front of him. That apparently gives him a feeling of safety and security. He stays there all day. They coax him into going to bed at night but even that's starting to become impossible as he just gets up and goes back to his place in the corner as soon as they leave him in bed."

Lily's eyes filled with tears at the memory of it all.  Winnie put her arms around Lily and held her as she cried. Winnie was glad they could be there for her, giving her the strength to be there for Joan.

"Hey, you put your arms around Lily but what about me, you don't do that for me," said Ted, wanting to lighten the mood.

"You're not upset, Lily is," retorted Winnie. "Anyway you have your cuddle in bed at night or had you forgotten."

"I hadn't forgotten but you call two minutes saying goodnight as a cuddle. You don't know what you are talking about woman."

"Oh don't I?" questioned Winnie, her eyes flashing dangerously.

Ted was starting to enjoy himself now. "Why do you think I look elsewhere for my cuddles. Lily here would like a cuddle I'm sure."

"Don't involve me in your argument," said Lily, but there was a smile on her face as she said it. Ted saw it and was pleased, that was exactly what he had hoped to see.

"Lily is it," said Winnie, with that look in her eye. "We'll see about that." She lifted her handbag and brought it down on Ted's head.

Lily burst out laughing, her worries about Joan put to one side for the moment. Ted and Winnie were pleased to see Lily's eyes light up with laughter. They nodded to each other, satisfied.

Lily dried her eyes and said, "Thank you both I really needed that."

"You're welcome," said Winnie. "Laughing always help when we are overwhelmed by problems."

"It certainly does, and you two are a real tonic."

"Anyway what about my cuddle then?" queried Ted.

"Your cuddle, do you want one from me or Lily?"

"I don't mind," replied Ted.

"Oh don't you," replied Winnie, lifting her handbag again and bringing it down on Ted's head.

"Oh no, not again," said Ted, rubbing his head.

"What do you expect, when you say things like that. I'm your woman no one else and don't you forget it," said Winnie with mock severity.

Lily just sat there smiling, enjoying the exchange. These two were definitely good for her, they always managed to cheer her up and make her laugh, however bad things seemed. They were a tonic, they really were. Where had they been all her life, if only she had known them earlier things could have been so different. Even now she couldn't help her memories drifting back to the past.

Ted noticed her eyes taking a faraway look and lifted his eyebrows at Winnie who too had noticed. They weren't sure how to bring her back to the present.

"Are you ok love?" queried Winnie.

"Sorry I was miles away, just wishing I had known you both earlier, everything could have been so different." Lily gave a sad smile.

"We may not have been around then but we are here for you now, you can talk to us about anything if that will help."

"Can I have a hug please?"

"Of course you can," said Winnie, enveloping Lily in her arms.

Lily stayed in those arms for some time, just enjoying being held by someone she knew loved her. She wished she could stay like that forever, but knew it had to end soon and she would have to go back to real life.

Eventually she pulled away from the embrace and smiled, this time a real smile which lit her whole face up. She had really needed that.

Ted and Winnie were pleased to see her back to normal again.

"Would you like another cuppa?" asked Ted.

"No thanks, I really must get going. I want to get back before the blackout."

Lily left her friends and started her journey home. She sat on the bus lost in thought so that she didn't register that someone had sat down next to her.

"Hello Lily,"

Lily jumped, startled before turning to look at Colin who had sat down next to her.

"Sorry didn't mean to make you jump. How are you doing?"

"I'm fine, just going home after visiting some friends," said Lily.

"Same here," said Colin, although that wasn't strictly true. He had been meeting with Eric again and it hadn't gone well. Eric was really getting suspicious about where his true loyalties lay. He would have to be very careful in future. He was there to do a job and that couldn't happen if he was found out, but at the same time how could he get the information he was after if Eric became suspicious. At the same time he wasn't ready to bring things to a close. If he pulled out now it would take ages for someone else to infiltrate the group and to be trusted. They didn't have that long, it was a matter of national security.

Colin and Lily sat in companionable silence, neither one knowing what to say. Lily hadn't forgotten the threat that Colin had seemed to make months ago and it made her wary of him. She didn't know what was really going on and she didn't want to know, it was obviously dangerous for her.

"Haven't seen you around much lately," said Colin, trying to make conversation.

"I've been there," said Lily abruptly, not wanting to get into conversation with Colin.

"How's your husband? I hope he has recovered now." Colin tried again.

"He's fine," responded Lily, still being very short with him, refusing to be drawn into conversation.

Colin gave up, seeing it was useless, she wasn't going to talk and he couldn't really blame her. He had been quite harsh with her that time, which he bitterly regretted, but needs must and there was a war on.

The silence continued until Lily came to her stop. "See you around," she said politely, before getting off the bus.

………

Lily and Joan were having lunch together, or rather Lily was eating but Joan was pushing the food around on the plate, her face ashen. Lily was worried about her friend, she had lost weight and was clearly not looking after herself.

"You've got to eat," said Lily, with a look of concern on her face. "You're not going to be any good to Arthur if you end up in hospital."

"I haven't any appetite since he went into that place," responded Joan dully.

"That's not all you are not doing though, you are very pale and you don't look as if you have washed your hair for ages," commented Lily. This was obvious as Joan's hair had a lacklustre appearance, no longer shining and properly shaped.

"There seems no point anymore, Arthur's not here to see me, so why bother."

"You've got to come out of this," said Lily sharply, wanting to shock her friend out of the depression she had sunk into.

"No point. What reason have I got to keep going? At least before, Arthur was with me in body even if not in his mind. I could at least pretend he would get better one day," said Joan flatly.

"You can't keep on like this, you're going to go down the same path as my mother. I won't allow it," retorted Lily, resorting to shock tactics with a hope of getting through to her friend.

"You don't understand," said Joan, on the verge of tears.

Lily was pleased to at least get some sort of emotional reaction from her friend. It was a good sign as prior to this chat Joan had spoken everything in a monotone.

"Don't I? Don't forget I lived with a mother who never recovered from my father's death. Also what about the worry I've had over Jack when I hadn't heard from him for ages and then when he was injured."

Joan had the grace to look ashamed of herself. Lily was right, she knew, but she wasn't ready to acknowledge it. Lily knew all that Joan was going through and did understand. She was wrong to shut her friend out. Lily was right she wasn't looking after herself, she had given up on life along with Arthur. Lily's words were a wake up call. She must force herself to keep carrying on. Joan picked up her fork, which lay on the plate and starting putting food in her mouth. She chewed but didn't really taste anything, but at least it was a start. There wasn't much substance to the food anyway, being vegetables with potato cooked in it like a soup. What she wouldn't give for some proper meat, but she must not think of that. Meat was a very scarce commodity these days.

Lily smiled to herself as she watched Joan finish her meal. She had definitely said something that got through to her friend. She hoped Joan would start taking care of herself now, even if in only small ways at first. Maybe they should get into the habit of eating together. Pooling their coupons might make a better meal for themselves.

**Chapter eleven**

"Heil Hitler!"

Lily gasped, quickly putting her hand over her mouth to smother the sound. Lily wanted to get away from there, she needed to think and if she were caught anywhere nearby it would be dangerous. Now she understood Colin's threats. She wasn't safe. Would Colin do anything to her? No, she didn't think so he would have done it by now if he was going to. Had anyone else heard the two men talking at any time, or was it just her? She always seemed to be in the wrong place at the wrong time. Unwittingly she had stumbled across traitors and here was she thinking it was all about the black market when all along it was far more serious. What should she do? Whom could she tell? They were all being warned to be careful because walls have ears. Something needed to be done, but who was safe?

"Shush," said Colin. "Do you want everyone to know who we are and what we're up to. I don't want to hang even if you do. We're traitors, but I'd rather no one knew that, I value my life even if you don't."

Eric looked at him severely. "You should be prepared to die for the Fatherland and our beloved Fuhrer, if you were really on our side," he said, giving Colin a shrewd look. He had used the Nazi greeting as a test to see how Colin would react. He was still unsure about Colin's loyalty. Maybe he should just dispose of him quietly. The man following Colin hadn't come up with anything suspicious but that didn't mean anything. Of course Colin would be careful, they were spies after all. He didn't realise that Colin had already guessed that he was being watched and had deliberately led the man on a merry dance.

Lily rushed back to the ward. She couldn't wait for the end of the shift so she could go home and think about what she had heard. She really wished she could discuss it with someone but she had to be so careful, no one could be trusted. If only Jack were here, he would know what to do. That was it, somehow she needed to get a message to him, but how? Over the phone wouldn't be any good because the people on the exchange would hear what was being said and no one could know what she had witnessed.

"Earth to Lily, earth to Lily," said the ward sister. "You've been elsewhere since you got back from your break. It's not like you. Is everything ok?"

"What? Sorry, I've got something on my mind and I'm unsure what to do."

"If you need to talk I'm here," said the sister. Lily was a good nurse and usually very focused.

"Thanks, but I'm sure I'll sort it out. I won't let it interfere with my work."

Lily tried to put what she had heard to the back of her mind for the rest of the shift. It wouldn't help for anyone to see how distracted she was, she couldn't let the wrong people become suspicious. She was very grateful when the shift finished and she could go home.

She was in the habit of dropping into Joan after work since that awful day when Arthur was institutionalised. Today Joan noticed how distracted Lily was which wasn't like Lily at all.

"Is everything all right?" Joan asked, concerned for her friend.

"I'm ok just thinking about something. I can't say anything at the moment, you know what they say, walls have ears." Lily was still mulling over what she had heard and wondering how to get word to Jack, for by now she felt sure Jack would be able to advise her on who to contact, for she knew she must do something, she couldn't keep this knowledge to herself. They were spies. She couldn't believe she had unwittingly uncovered spies, it was the sort of thing one sees at the pictures not something that happened in real life, but here she was in that situation and she had to deal with it. They couldn't get away with it any longer, there was no telling how much damage they were doing to the country.

"You haven't heard a word I said have you?" said Joan, a bit put out.

Lily gave herself a shake and said, "Sorry, I was miles away. Something came up at work and I can't get it out of my mind. I am still wondering what to do about it."

"Are you sure you don't want to talk about it, it might help."

"It's tricky, I really need to talk to Jack, he might know what to do, but it isn't safe to write to him as I can't allow it to fall into the wrong hands."

"Sounds mysterious," said Joan, intrigued by her friend's words.

"Sorry I can't tell you but the fewer who know about it the safer it is."

"Now you have me worried. If it is that serious then you should maybe ring the base and try to speak to Jack and arrange to meet him somewhere quiet."

"That's a good idea I'll try that. Thank you. Now that is enough of my problems, how are you and how's Arthur, you went to see him today didn't you?"

Joan looked glum and her eyes filled with tears.

"I take it things are not good," said Lily, putting her hand on Joan's arm as a gesture of support.

Joan shook her head, unable to speak as the tears slid down her cheeks. Her eyes were already bright red like blood which told Lily these were not the first tears she had cried that day. The tear stained cheeks and quivering lips should have told her how distraught her friend was. She felt guilty for being so caught up in her own problems that she had failed to see Joan's obvious distress when she arrived.

Joan sniffed and wiped her eyes. "He was violent again. He had another patient held by the throat with his arm, threatening to cut his throat with a knife. He was so convinced the patient was the enemy. When I got there he was in bed sedated."

"I'm so sorry, that doesn't sound good, but he's in the best place, they know how to deal with this sort of situation."

"They told me if it happens again he will have to be kept sedated."

"Oh Joan, I am so sorry it's bad news."

"When I got there they took me to the office and told me all this. I started shaking and crying when they told me, but they were really good, they got me a cup of tea to try to calm me down. It just seems so awful. I know they have to think of the safety of everyone, staff and patients, but I can't bear the thought of him being constantly sedated."

"I know it's hard, but I'm sure they wouldn't do it if it wasn't absolutely necessary," said Lily, trying to offer some comfort to her friend. She knew, however, that there was little comfort to be had in this situation. It was just another tragic story of the damage war does to people.

"I know what you're saying is right. I just don't want to accept it of my Arthur. In my head he's still the man I fell in love with, the man before the Great War destroyed him."

"That's understandable, you love him and what's happening now is the grieving process, because the situation is forcing you to recognise that he is not that man anymore and never will be again."

Joan sighed, she knew her friend was right but was struggling to accept it and the latest incident was more evidence that the man she loved had gone forever.

They sat in silence for a while, there was nothing to say. Lily felt Joan's misery but couldn't find any more words of comfort. What could be said that would help? There was nothing except to be there with Joan, sharing the suffering and grief in some small way. Yes, that was all she could do for her.

Joan dried her eyes and managed a weak smile. "I'll be fine," she said.

Lily left Joan with a heavy heart but for now she had her own problem to think about. She decided to try and contact Jack the next day, there was nothing she could do for now. She went to her own home and shut the door. The silence seemed menacing today as she continued to ruminate on what she had heard. She locked all the doors and closed the blackout, it made her feel safer somehow. She didn't really believe she was at risk at the moment because no one knew what she had overheard, but the air still seemed filled with tension and a shiver of something, maybe fear went through her. She didn't believe she would feel safe until Colin and Eric were arrested and removed from society.

She had no appetite due to the tension she felt. It was as if she had to look over her shoulder all the time, expecting danger but not knowing when or if it would show itself. She forced herself to eat a slice of toast but struggled with nausea as she tried to chew and swallow it. She didn't expect to sleep that night but knew she had to try or she would be too tired to talk coherently in the morning when she contacted Jack. She lay in bed going over and over what she had heard. Was there any way she could have misunderstood? Was it just a nightmare from which she would awake from? No, that wasn't the case, it was real and she couldn't possibly have heard wrong when the Nazi greeting had been given very clearly. She couldn't believe that they could be stupid enough to give that greeting in England in a public place. Anyone could have overheard. It was such a great risk they were taking, and it would be that greeting that would lead to their exposure and capture.

The next morning she dressed quickly and went to the end of the street where she could phone the air base and hopefully speak to Jack.

"Hello can I possibly speak to Jack, it's his wife Lily and it's very urgent…. Yes if you could it would be great, thanks."

There was a pause while she waited for Jack to come on the line.

"Hello? Lily? Is everything ok? Nothing has happened to Bobby has it?"

"Oh Jack, I can't believe it's you. I don't know what to do, I'm in a difficult situation that is extremely serious and dangerous. It's concerning national security. I can't discuss it over the phone in case we are overheard, but I do need to speak to you as soon as possible. I don't know how to deal with it or who I should be contacting."

"Ok, slow down, it's going to be all right. Can you give me some sort of idea of what we are talking about?"

"Not really, it would be dangerous if the wrong person overheard us."

"Ok, ok, calm down and I'll see if I can get a pass to come and see you and we can talk it over. I'm sure when we talk it over things won't seem so bad."

"They won't seem better, this is really dire, I can't explain the seriousness of the situation. I'm worried I may already be saying too much."

There was a pause while Jack spoke to someone in the background. He came back on the line, "I can't get a pass but if there is any way you could get down here I would be able to get a few hours off for us to meet somewhere away from the base so we can talk."

"Yes I think I could do that. I'm not working today so could catch the next train down there."

Lily put the phone down and breathed a sigh of relief. It was no longer her problem to solve herself. Jack would know what to do and the awful situation would be resolved correctly. She still found it hard to believe it was really happening, but it was and she had taken the first step to resolving it and ensuring the capture of two spies.

She rushed around getting ready for the trip. She felt slightly lighter now knowing the burden would soon be lifted off her shoulders. On her way she knocked on Joan's door to let her know where she was going.

"Good," said Joan on hearing what Lily had to say. "I hope he will be able to help and advise you on whatever is on your mind." If truth be told Joan felt a bit put out. She had always been there for Lily and she thought they were close friends but here they were and Lily was not confiding in her, saying she couldn't tell her. Could it be that their friendship wasn't as intimate as she had thought?

"I'm sorry I can't tell you what it is," said Lily. "You'll know all about it when it is over and then you will understand why I am reluctant to say anything."

Joan smiled, slightly mollified by Lily's response. "That's fine, just go and get it sorted out." They embraced and then Lily was gone.

.........

Lily arrived at the nearest stop to the air base approximately two hours later. It had been an uneventful journey which Lily was relieved about, although she still found herself looking over her shoulder ever watchful of danger. She didn't think she would feel safe again until Eric and Colin had been caught. When she hadn't been looking over her shoulder she looked at the countryside speeding past. All the green fields, luscious grass everywhere with hedgerows, again a lovely colour with wild flowers growing, creating a pleasant variety of colours. As Lily looked at the scenery she thought how different it was, here it was totally undisturbed by the ravages of war that was turning towns and cities to rubble. Trees overshadowing the green fields, tall and imposing. How beautiful it all was. Lily would have enjoyed it more if her mind had been free. It was so peaceful and tranquil watching the scenery go by, undisturbed by anything.

She decided to walk to the air base where she was to meet Jack, before going off somewhere secluded where they wouldn't be overheard.

When Jack appeared they embraced, unwilling to let the other go. Jack was the first to let go and held Lily at arms length. He could see in her eyes that something serious was bothering her. He knew his Lily well and was able to pick up even the slightest nuance. She was frowning although probably unaware of this.

"Come on, we can go this way, we can talk as we go or would you rather wait until we reach the small shack I had in mind. It is empty and doesn't belong to anyone so we will be undisturbed there."

Lily gave a small nod, not knowing what to say. Now she was here she wondered if she was making a mountain out of a molehill. Maybe it wasn't as serious as she thought and there was an innocent explanation. It wasn't in her to exaggerate or imagine things though so she thought it must be real.

They walked along in silence hand in hand, just enjoying each others company until the time came when that peace would be shattered by the information she held.

"Here we are," said Jack, slowing down and letting go of Lily's hand. He pushed open the door and stood aside, ever the gentleman, ushering Lily in first.

They sat on the floor as there were no chairs, in fact there wasn't anything, it was completely empty. It was only a small area inside Lily noticed in the dim light, they had left the door slightly ajar to allow a bit of light to enter, not wanting to be in complete darkness.

They sat in silence at first, Lily unsure how to start. Should she start at the beginning with the little things she had overheard or start with the greeting that had panicked her so much. The early things though seemed inconsequential in themselves but put together with the Nazi greeting seemed so much more sinister. In the end she decided to tell Jack everything right from the beginning. She paused after telling him of Colin's threat to her. It all seemed so long ago now, but still fresh in her mind.

"Why didn't you tell me back then?" asked Jack, trying to work things out in his head as to what all this meant.

"To be honest I didn't take much notice, I thought it was some black market thing he'd got involved in." Lily continued with the story until Jack knew everything.

Jack gave a deep sigh and sat in silence for a few minutes, trying to work it all out in his mind. There was no doubt that his wife had stumbled across something very serious and dangerous and he needed the time to think.

Lily sat tense and apprehensive in the silence, waiting for Jack's reaction.

After a while he spoke. "I'm glad you came to me and kept it to yourself. Something definitely has to be done but I'm not sure who we can trust."

Lily sighed with relief, it was no longer hers to bear the burden.

"Look, I tell you what, I'll have a word with the squadron leader, he's good. I trust him and he'll know what to do. If you wait here I'll see if he can come and have a chat with you. It would be better if it came first hand from you as he may have questions. I don't want to risk getting some of the detail wrong and messing up everything. It has to be completely accurate if we are to help capture them."

Lily nodded in agreement and Jack left, promising to be back as soon as possible. On her own Lily leaned her head against the side of the shack and let her mind drift back over everything she had heard. If in some ways she had misunderstood then she was going to destroy lives. This was serious and was a matter of life or death. Could she really be sure they were traitors and working for the Third Reich. She lifted her hand up to her hair and twirled it in her fingers, a habit she had when she was uncertain. Surely though she wouldn't have heard the Nazi greeting if it wasn't. No one would use that greeting in fun, not in these days. No, she had to have it right. She hoped Jack would be back soon with his superior, she was anxious to have it taken out of her hands. She twisted her hair around her finger, unaware of what she was doing. She stood up and nervously paced the floor of the shack. Backwards and forwards she went over the small ground. She regularly glanced at the door to see if anyone was approaching, but nothing. She hoped Jack would return soon but she had to give him a chance to tell his superior what the situation was. She heard footsteps approaching hurriedly and with purpose. The door was pushed open and Jack appeared with another man in tow.

"This is Squadron Leader Jackson," he said by way of introduction.

Lily shook the proffered hand. The squadron leader was a heavy built man with wisps of grey hair on a nearly bald scalp. He had a firm handshake which left Lily feeling bruised.

"Well young woman, Jack has told me quite a tale but I'd like to hear it from you. This is a very serious matter we have here," he said sternly.

Lily found herself quaking under his steely gaze but she had to speak to him and then leave it to his judgement. She related the story just as she had to Jack. The squadron leader left her to tell her story without interruption.

"Hmm," he said with a thoughtful expression on his face when she had finished. "We certainly do have a situation here. You did the right thing coming down and speaking to young Jack here." He paused before continuing, "Why didn't you say something sooner, as soon as you overheard the first conversation?"

"I was only hearing fragments of a conversation and thought they were just involved in the black market. Yes, I know that's illegal as well but I didn't want to get involved. When Colin threatened me I just wanted to keep quiet and not bring any further attention to myself. It's only now that I realise it's more serious and can no longer stay quiet." She looked at the floor, feeling foolish and not able to look into the eyes of this rather austere man. Eyes that were watery, pale blue and as cold as ice. She hoped Jack was right in trusting this man because she really didn't like him and found him overbearing and intimidating.

"Well, I have to take this seriously. I need to make a phone call to a mate of mine in the government. He will know what to do. We need this to be sorted out straight away before any more damage can be done." He spoke this in staccato sentences which made Lily shiver.

"I'll get Lily booked in somewhere in case she's needed further. I'm not comfortable with her travelling back to London at a late hour."

They all left the shack. Lily was still tense and anxious, despite the situation now being out of her hands and squadron leader Jackson had done nothing to allay her fears. Jack took her hand and gave it a squeeze saying, "You did the right thing you know and the squadron leader is really a good guy. Underneath that gruff exterior he's a nice man that really cares about those under his command."

"If you say so," commented Lily, still not sure.

Jack got Lily booked into a small hotel for the night. It was a very plain room with nothing attractive about it.  Green walls and a bed that looked as if it had seen better days. When Lily sat on it, it sagged underneath her. Oh well, it was only for the night, she could put up with it that long. It had been agreed that they would meet at the shack in the morning so they could hear what was going to happen or if there were any more questions Lily needed to answer.

Lily spent a sleepless night, tossing and turning on the lumpy mattress, unable to switch her thoughts off. She just kept going over it again and again, round and round in circles. What would they say or do? How would they catch them? It was only luck that she had overheard any of their conversation, or should that be bad luck for her! She didn't want anyone put in danger but it seemed as if the hospital could be put at risk as that is where they worked. Was it possible to catch them elsewhere? Maybe it needed to be where they were together though so no one would be alerted, after all they didn't know how many were involved, there must be others.

She dozed off eventually when it started to get light and awoke at the knock on her door. She roused herself enough to get out of bed and open it.  Jack stood there, a serious expression on his face that changed to concern when he saw the tousled hair and sleepy look on his wife's face.

"Are you ok?"

"Not sure, give me a minute to wake up, I didn't sleep much, everything just kept going round and round in my mind, but I still came up with no conclusion."

Jack put his arm around his wife and said, "You don't have to keep going over it any more, you passed it to me and I passed it to Jackson. It's in his hands now. Come on, get dressed then we must go back to the shack and meet him. He should have news by now. I said I'd come for you and he would make his own way there, it's safer that way so no one starts questioning what's going on."

Lily was ready quickly. A quick wash and brush of her hair. She had been so late waking that she didn't have time to do her hair properly so it still looked like a spiky hedgehog.

They walked quickly to the shack hand in hand in companionable silence. Squadron Leader Jackson was already there, pacing up and down with impatience.

He didn't waste time on pleasantries, just getting straight to the matter at hand. "Well, I have spoken to someone high up who is taking the matter very seriously for this situation is a threat against national security. I'm not giving any names as it's safer that way if no one knows. He advises you don't go back to work for a few days until this is over. He doesn't know exactly how long it will take to resolve, but he's getting straight on to it. He has sources that he can plug into who will hopefully get him more detailed information. You said they were Eric and Colin didn't you? Porters in the hospital?"

Lily nodded, no words would come out. It was out of her hands completely now, but she felt no relief, just blank. "I don't know if I can take time off though."

"You should try as we don't know how things will turn out, they could get dangerous. Unfortunately we can't speak to the matron for you because it would be admitting something was happening and we don't want anyone else knowing anything. We can't risk the two men finding out anything and also we don't know if there is anyone else in the hospital in on this. There are questions that need to be thought about such as why are they at the hospital in the first place and not in a military hospital. It's all very odd. My source seems to think there are more people involved who maybe report to these two. Ideally they would infiltrate the group and try and find out who's at the top of the chain and in contact with Germany, but because of what you overheard we have to act quicker. Colin already knows you know something so to do nothing could put you in further danger. These are very dangerous men we're talking about and I can't emphasise more fully that you really should avoid going back to work. You would have to make some excuse to avoid it. You must also say nothing to anyone else, do you understand?"

"Yes sir," said Lily quietly. "I'm not sure I can avoid work though and surely it would be better if I am there. If I don't turn up when expected won't that cause suspicion to arise especially as Colin knows I have heard them?"

"We didn't think of that," admitted Jackson, after some thought. "Our main concern was for your safety and the safety of others, but you have a point, it may look more suspicious if you don't turn up, but there is the other side of the argument as well, that you could arouse suspicion if you can't avoid letting others know something is worrying you. You would only have to be a bit distracted and people will start asking questions and that could alert the very people we don't want to. I hope that makes sense?"

Lily nodded but still stubbornly clung to the thought that it would be better for her to continue going to work.

"I really think you should listen to the squadron leader and superiors in the government. They know what they're doing and I don't want you in any danger. Ideally you wouldn't be involved at all, but you are and have done the right thing speaking out, but now you need to take their advice," said Jack with a concerned expression on his face.

"I understand what you're saying," said Lily, looking up at her handsome husband. "I'll only go stir crazy at home wondering what is happening at the hospital. Also we must remember Colin knows where I live so surely I would be safer at the hospital where I am surrounded by others most of the time."

"How does he know where you live?" asked Jackson sharply.

"He helped me take my neighbour and her husband home after they had some bad news," said Lily briefly, not wanting to go into detail about the loss they had just had.

"That changes everything then," said Jackson. "I'd better get back to my source and let him know this and seek further advice. You two wait here, I'll be back as soon as I can."

He left the shack and hurried off.

Jack and Lily turned to look at each other. Lily was on the verge of tears. Jack put his arm around her to comfort her, but truth be told he was very anxious about her. He wished she had never heard anything and that Colin hadn't seen her. He hoped she would be able to stay safe wherever she was. He wished with all his heart that she could stay down there near him until this whole mess was over, but he had to be on the base and would be unable to be with her so she would be all alone. The thought suddenly occurred to him that maybe they would have someone following her and then she could be in more danger because they would know where she was and guess what she was up to. He shivered, determined not to let Lily realise what his thoughts now were, he didn't want to frighten her any more than she already was. He would mention it to Jackson though. He wished there was some way of giving her some protection but doubted that would happen. This could get very bad indeed.

They paced the floor wishing Jackson would come back quickly. Lily, as much as she disliked the man, was dependent on him now for her safety and the safety of the staff and patients at the hospital, not only that but the country's safety. Nazism was evil and no one wanted it to spread to England.

It seemed like forever waiting for Jackson to return. They spent most of the time silent, each lost in their own thoughts, not willing to reveal what they were thinking. It was in fact a couple of hours before Jackson returned. They heard his footsteps before they saw him. He seemed to stamp as he drew near as if marching like a soldier, with military precision.

When he appeared he got straight to the point. "Well, my contact, now he has this new information agrees it might be best to carry on with your usual routine Lily, going to work and carrying on as usual. That seems the safest thing to do. No one wants you in more danger than you already are, but you must take precautions, be aware at all times. It's imperative you avoid that part of the hospital where you have overheard them talking, we can't risk you being seen again. You will have to stay focused at all times, not distracted, as anyone could pick up on that and start wondering and if our men notice then it will put you in immediate danger as they could put two and two together. Do you think you can do that?"

Lily gave a nod of her head, not sure what to say. She just hoped she could carry it off.

"Good girl," said Jackson with what could pass as a smile, a slight upturn of the lips. He noticed Jack was looking worried and determined to have a word with him when they were alone. He didn't want to worry Lily any further but he was still concerned himself. This was a dangerous business and he wished Lily had never discovered it. There was a very vulnerable side to her.

"I'll take Lily to the station so she can catch the train back to London and then I'll come straight back to base," said Jack.

Jackson nodded, and said, "Come to me as soon as you get back." He lifted his eyebrows and glanced briefly at Lily trying to get the message across to Jack that he wanted to speak to him privately without Lily present.

Jack got the silent message and gave a nod in understanding.

Jack saw Lily on to the train and rushed back to base, eager to chat with Jackson.

"I'm worried," said Jack as soon as the door was shut. "It occurred to me that they might be following her since Colin knows where she lives and knows she overheard them, surely they would take precautions to ensure no one found out about them. These are very dangerous individuals."

"Calm down," said Jackson quietly, "We have already thought of that which is why it's best to stick to her usual routine so anyone following won't get suspicious."

"But they would already be suspicious with her rushing down here won't they."

"Possibly, but there is nothing we can do about that. She did the right thing and she kept her mouth shut so we think she'll be ok. Anyway they are going to try and arrange protection for her. You have to trust them to know what they are doing. They will keep a discreet eye on her. It will only be for a few days anyway."

Jack still looked worried with his brow furrowed and his mouth set in a straight line as if he was gritting his teeth, which if truth be known he was. He was very worried about his wife and Jackson hadn't succeeded in allaying his fears. The only thing to stop him worrying would be for this whole affair to be over and the enemy caught.

What no one knew was the government knew about the traitors in the hospital. They were keeping an eye on them, wanting to know who was the boss and who all the members were. It was more widespread than the hospital they knew, but so far didn't know where and whom. Unfortunately with Lily having heard them it precipitated things and they had to act sooner.

..........

Lily soon arrived back in London, still a worried look on her face. The enormity of what she knew was still inside her head and she couldn't let it go completely. She hadn't noticed the countryside as it sped by. She hadn't even noticed the rubble of war torn London when she arrived back. She went straight home, she even avoided knocking on Joan's door immediately as she didn't feel she could cope with Joan's problems at the moment. She needed time alone to think, fortunately she wasn't working until tomorrow so she could have a long rest.

She was scared, more scared than she had admitted. On stumbling across the two traitors she was out of her depth completely. She couldn't wait until it was all over and the gang caught, then maybe she could relax and put it behind her. How safe was she really she wondered? She tried arguing with herself, telling herself that if they were going to do anything to her they would have done so before now, as it had been ages since Colin had made the threat to her. This rational side of her couldn't win over the other side of her brain that knew she was in grave danger. They knew they had been overheard so anything could happen at any time.

She really wasn't feeling comfortable on her own, she jumped at the slightest sound, convinced they had come for her. When there was a knock at the door she let out a scream, it was happening, they were there. She curled herself in a ball to try and protect herself. It was an instinctive reaction.

"Lily are you there? Are you all right?" Joan called when she got no answer to her knock, but sure she had heard a noise from inside.

"Keep away, keep away," cried Lily, terrified and unable to realise it was her friend at the door.

"Lily, it's me, Joan, can you let me in, I'm worried."

Lily took a minute to let the words seep into her brain and gave herself a shake, she really must stop this or she would be causing suspicion and alerting Eric and Colin and whoever else might be involved. She stood up and went to the door. "Hello," she said, somewhat sheepishly, feeling foolish now.

"Is everything ok? I heard you scream when I knocked," asked Joan concerned, with good reason as Lily was very pale and there was a look of fear on her face. She stood very rigid, not responding to Joan's hug.

"Everything is fine," she said at last, trying to convince herself as much as Joan.

"You are not persuading me, you are pale and looking frightened. Even someone who doesn't know you would see you're not all right."

Lily tried to shake herself out of it, not very successfully. She wished she could have stayed with Jack. This wasn't going to work, she didn't think she would be able to carry on as normal, she was too jumpy, and very scared.

"Is there something wrong with Jack?" asked Joan, trying to get something out of her friend.

"No, he's fine,"

"There must be something, you are not your usual self," replied Joan, despairing of finding out what was bothering Lily. She obviously didn't want to say.

"I can't say anything at the moment, sorry, you'll find out eventually though, when it's all over."

"Sounds intriguing," said Joan, totally mystified as to why Lily couldn't say anything. What was going on?

"Anyway do you want a cuppa?" asked Lily, trying to behave normally and wanting to change the subject.

"I thought you'd never ask," said Joan.

Lily put the kettle on and they sat in companionable silence waiting for the kettle to boil.

The tea made, they sat at the table. Lily picked up the tea pot to pour the hot, insipid liquid into the cups but Joan stopped her, saying, "I'll do that, your hands are shaking and we don't want to waste any, with tea being as scarce as it is."

Lily gave in seeing the sense in what Joan said, she definitely wasn't herself. She was just grateful her friend was no longer prying. She felt guilty keeping this to herself but she couldn't say anything.

Joan tried to think of something to say but was struggling as Lily didn't seem willing to talk and she wasn't going to say what was going on with her. Going to see Jack obviously hadn't done any good as she seemed worse than when she went away.

"I bet it was good to see Jack and be out of the city for a while," said Joan eventually, not knowing what else to say. She didn't want to say anything about her situation as it was obvious Lily wasn't in the right frame of mind to hear her problems, she looked as if she had the weight of the world on her shoulders.

"Yes," said Lily shortly, not going into any detail.

Joan struggled again, what could she say when Lily was reluctant to talk about anything? "Do you want me to leave?" asked Joan eventually, wondering if it was best to leave Lily to her thoughts.

Lily paled further, "No, no please stay. I'm sorry I'm not good company at the moment. A lot on my mind. I'd like you to stay it will take my mind off things."

Joan nodded, hearing the desperation in Lily's voice. Something was very wrong she knew. She felt helpless as there was nothing she could do if Lily wouldn't or couldn't say what was going on. They sat in silence, both lost in their own thoughts.

"How is Arthur?" asked Lily, trying to put all thoughts of traitors out of her mind and concentrate on her friend for a while.


Joan looked sombre and replied, "About the same, he still shows some aggression towards others which is worrying and he is being kept sedated. When it wears off he can become aggressive again. He is just completely lost in the past and not in a good way. There is no reasoning with him, he sees himself as the only person for the allies everyone else is the enemy coming for him in the trenches."

Lily was still only half listening and said, "Sorry I'm not good company today. My mind is elsewhere."

"I can see that, I wish you could tell me what is going on it might help."

"When it's over I'll tell you everything but for now I can't say anything. Jack knows about it and the situation is being dealt with appropriately. I don't think I will relax until it is over."

..........

Lily turned up for her shift as usual, hoping she will be able to focus on the job and not think about the situation. She wandered around in a bit of a daze, coming out of it only when someone spoke her name a couple of times. She was getting some funny looks from other nurses. This was not like her at all. She was a good nurse, very popular with everyone.

"I'm sorry sister," she said after being spoken too twice as she had forgotten to check on post op patients.

"Is everything all right?" asked the ward sister. "This is so unlike you."

"Everything is fine, or it will be," replied Lily vaguely.

When she was supposed to go to the stock room she went a different way not wanting to pass where Colin and Eric usually met, she didn't want to hear anything else. She really didn't know what she was supposed to do for the best. Maybe she should have stayed away, but it had been decided she should continue as normal so that is what she was trying to do. When she got back to the ward she found Matron was asking to see her.

With much trepidation she knocked on Matron's door opening it slowly, almost peeping around it as she entered.

"Well come in then," said Matron sternly.

Lily was confronted by not just Matron but a gentleman she had never met. He stood up as she entered, towering over her, he took his hat off and held his hand out to shake hers. "Take a seat," he said.

She sat down, still worried as to what this was all about. She had a suspicion it was to do with Colin and Eric.

"Hello, I am Major Whitmarsh. I am here to talk about the traitors you stumbled across by chance. Could you go through again what you have heard and seen. Don't miss anything out."

Lily looked at Matron, unsure whether she should say anything or not in front of her. This could be a trap set for her.

"It's all right," said the Major trying to reassure her. "We've had to inform Matron of everything that is happening as we're hoping to capture them tomorrow. She needed to know what was going on in her hospital and what is going to happen."

Lily gave a slight nod of her head and again told the story from beginning to end. She left nothing out, even describing her trip down to see Jack and what had been discussed then.

"You did the right thing," said the Major reassuringly. "It's actually a bit of a tricky case as we have no time to find out more information about them and to try to find out who else is involved, but we feel it has to end now so as not to put you in more danger than you already are."

Lily shuddered.

"There has been someone assigned to watch you and make sure you're safe at all times until this is over. Matron tells me the two men are on shift tomorrow together so we intend making our move then. Depending on how it turns out we may have to ask you to identify them as the two men you overheard, but we hope it won't come to that. We don't want you in more danger than you already are. In fact from our point of view we're sorry you are involved in any way."

"I'm not sure I can continue as normal as agreed when I first told my husband and was given that advice. I am distracted by it and it is being noticed on the ward."

"In that case it might be better if you went home. Don't worry you'll be safe, you won't be alone, but you won't see anyone either. We are very good at our job and know how to follow without being seen. We have to be in these days of war and spies."

Matron also gave permission for Lily to leave early. She was meant to be on an early shift the next day but was swapped to a late so she could be there if needed when the capture was to take place.

Lily was glad to be leaving. To be quite honest she didn't feel safe at work at the moment, anything could happen. Now she knew what was really going on Colin's threat seemed very sinister.

She caught the bus to go home but kept looking around nervously wondering if her protector was on the bus with her or if there were any traitors watching and waiting to get to her. She knew she would probably never know. Knowing there was someone looking out for her didn't make her feel very safe though.

She looked out of the window trying to focus on something else instead of her fears. She saw all the rubble of bombed buildings, the people walking by looking down at the ground, bowed down by care and despair. Worn out and fed up with the war that seemed never ending. They were also looking down, needing to be careful where they walked with bricks and people's belongings everywhere from the bombed buildings, careful not to trip over anything. It seemed to Lily as if the city had been completely destroyed as it lay desolate and ruined.

She got off the bus and began the walk home. She had the feeling that someone was following her. She was sure footsteps could be heard from behind her. They were only soft foot falls but she was certain, or was it her imagination because of all that was happening. She stopped, pretending to look in her bag for something. She listened but heard nothing so she continued walking. There it was again, the sound of footsteps. She stopped and looked cautiously around. There was no one that she could see and the footsteps had stopped. Was she so sensitive that her own footsteps were frightening her? She remained on high alert until she arrived home, and again before going inside she looked all around her to make sure she was safe. There was a vague, frightening thought that maybe there would be someone waiting inside to kill her. What would they do to her? Would she be tortured and then killed or would they just kill her? What would happen to Bobby and Jack if anything happened to her? Who would look after Bobby after the war, that's if this blinking war ever finished. She smiled to herself as she used Winnie's favourite word. What would happen to them? They would be devastated if anything happened to her she knew. They had become very close over the months. She wished they were with her right now, not because she wanted them in danger too but because Winnie would be able to hit them over the head with her handbag. Just thinking about this made Lily smile. Winnie could win the war single handed with her handbag, lethal as it was!

She shut the door behind her and checked all the rooms just to make sure. Yes, the house was empty, except for her. She didn't feel completely safe however. They would have ways of getting in if they wanted to. She looked at the poker near the fire and thought of keeping that by her side with intention of using it if necessary, at least it might make her feel safer. The poker was heavy and used on any intruder would definitely knock them out or more likely kill them. She, as a nurse was unhappy about hurting anyone but it was a matter of life or death and she wanted to be the one to have life. Her family needed her and she wasn't happy to leave this world just yet. She collapsed into a chair with a sigh. She hoped this would all be over soon, she didn't think she would feel safe until then. In the meantime she kept the poker beside her, ready to use it if necessary. She found she couldn't even eat anything, sick with apprehension. She closed the blackout curtains but that made her feel worse because she couldn't see if anyone was nearby. She was jumping at every shadow she saw outside, even though it was usually perfectly innocent, a neighbour going about their business.

That night she tossed and turned and kept leaning out of bed to be reassured by the feel of the poker on the floor next to the bed. The slightest creak had her fearful. If she didn't stop this soon she would be joining Arthur she thought with a wry smile. She was certainly going round the bend with all this, all her senses on high alert, even when there was no evidence anyone was going to do anything. Anyway, there was supposed to be someone nearby looking out for her so she should be safe. Was it them she could hear when she thought she was being followed? She wasn't convinced because they had said she wouldn't know anyone was there as they were very good at their job.

She got up very early giving up on the idea of sleep, she felt safer downstairs although she was fearful going downstairs absolutely convinced there was someone behind her waiting to push her down the stairs. She kept looking, holding the poker as if her life depended on it, which it might well do. There was no one there and logically she knew there couldn't be anyone as she would have heard if anyone had broken in and there had been no one there when she had arrived home the previous day. Sitting very tense and still she tried sipping the tepid tea she had made. She needed something but she almost choked on every swallow. She tried a slice of toast but found it impossible to manage, retching on every mouthful. She felt guilty leaving it considering the lack of food in the shops but just couldn't eat anything. Anxiety was really getting to her. She wished she didn't have to go to work but since they had rearranged her shift so she would be there to identify the men if needed she had no choice.

There was a knock at the door, she stiffened, who could it be at this early hour? Would any attacker knock at the door like that, probably not, that just didn't make any sense. She got up, taking the poker with her. She opened the door, her hand raised with the poker ready to bring it down on someone's head.

"For heaven's sake, Lily, what are you doing with that thing." Joan said, taking a step back quickly.

Lily looked sheepish as she lowered the poker. "Sorry, I wasn't expecting you."

"Clearly," said Joan, dryly. "I just came to see if you were ok since you haven't been yourself lately, but I have my answer you're not all right."

Lily shook her head, the effort of keeping going as if nothing was happening was too much, a sleepless night had only made everything worse. She turned away, not wanting Joan to see her eyes shining bright with tears. Too late, Joan had seen.

She put her arms around Lily and held her, saying, "It will be ok whatever it is that's bothering you. I'm here for you. I'm sure it can't be anything too much." She looked closely at her friend seeing purple shadows under her eyes and came to the right conclusion. "Did you get any sleep last night? You look terrible."

"Thanks," said Lily, who in normal circumstances might have laughed at this, but laughter was very far from her mind at the moment. "It should all be over later today," she said.

"Come on, let's get you inside and sitting down. I'll make you a cup of tea, everything will seem better then."

Lily shook her head, "I've just tried to eat and drink but just couldn't manage it."

"You can't go to work in this state, you look like one of the patients," said Joan.

"I have no choice I have to," said Lily, wishing she could stay at home all day and avoid what was happening.

"I'll phone in sick for you,"

Lily looked defeated as she replied, "I have to go in they have specifically said they need me."

"You're no use to anyone like this," said Joan.

"You don't understand, I am the only one who can do it."

"You are right, I don't understand. Please, can't you tell me what is going on."

Lily shook her head, unable to speak. How she wished she could confide in her friend, but it had been impressed upon her that no one was to be told anything and she had to keep to that. Besides she didn't want her friend in danger as well and what could she do even if she did say anything. No, it had to be kept to herself.

Lily stood up, swaying slightly from the lack of sleep. Joan reacted quickly and held her friend, helping her back in the chair. "There is no way you can go to work like this. You'll end up in a bed yourself. You're no use to anyone like this. Look I know you say you have to go in," said Joan seeing Lily about to protest, "But why don't you go and have a lie down, maybe you will doze off. I'll stay here so you can rest easy."

Lily looked gratefully at her friend, "Thank you, I think I will, I didn't get any sleep last night."

Joan helped her friend up the stairs and got her settled into bed. Keeping her word she stayed with Lily and was satisfied when her eyes closed and she fell asleep.

………..

Lily was running, but she couldn't run fast enough. They were gaining on her rapidly. She could hear the footsteps behind her, getting closer all the time. Lily tried to scream but couldn't, no sound would come out. She knew she was in deadly peril but couldn't do anything about it, there was no escape. She was surrounded, there was running feet from every direction. What could she do? There was no help to be had. She stopped, having nowhere to run too. She wanted to slump down to the pavement but couldn't, that would make it easier for them to get her.

"We have been looking for you everywhere. Did you really think you could avoid us?" asked a voice in a strong German accent.

Lily tried to speak but again no sound would come out.

"Well you can not run now, we have you," said the voice again. He grabbed her and putting his hands around her throat started to squeeze hard.

Lily flailed around, fighting for every breath, thinking of Jack and Bobby and wondering how they would manage without her.

"Lily, Lily wake up," said Joan.

Lily's eyes flew open, terror obvious. "It's ok, you're having a bad dream. I'm here, you're safe."

Lily looked around her still terrified but wanting to believe she was safe. She was still in bed and Joan was by her side, other than the two of them the room was empty. She breathed a sigh of relief and relaxed a bit. Joan was relieved to see it. Whatever was bothering her friend was bad to be causing nightmares like that.

"I thought they had caught me," said Lily in a quiet voice, so quiet that Joan had to lean forward to catch what said.

"Who?" asked Joan.

"The people who are after me, they were going to kill me because of what I heard."

"What did you hear?" asked Joan, understandably confused. "Maybe I should get a doctor out, you're not well." Joan looked at Lily's bright eyes and placed her hand on her forehead to see if she had a temperature. "You're hot, I should get a doctor."

"No, no I'm fine," said Lily. "It was just a bad dream as you said. Now I'm awake I'll be fine, you'll see. I'm a nurse and I don't feel ill."

Joan shook her head slowly. She didn't feel Lily was in the best place to judge her state of health. Joan was worried about her friend, frown lines deepening in her forehead as she looked at Lily.

"Really, I'll be fine," said Lily, seeing her friend was unconvinced. "I thought they were after me and caught me."

"Who?" asked Joan.

"The Nazis," replied Lily, realising she wasn't making much sense.

"I really think I should call a doctor," repeated Joan.

Lily shook her head, "No, I'll be fine," she said, not convincing Joan.

"Maybe you are under too much pressure and need a few days off to rest," said Joan, still worried about her friend.

"No, no it's not like that. It's real."

"It was just a bad dream. I still think you're unwell and should see a doctor."

Lily was adamant she didn't need a doctor. She couldn't explain to Joan although she realised she was giving too much away. Fortunately Joan was convinced it was a nightmare and nothing more, with no bearing on reality.

"I must get up. I have to get ready for work."

Joan shook her head but knew it was pointless trying to persuade Lily otherwise. In her mind her friend wasn't fit for work. Something was obviously very wrong and had been for a few days, ever since Lily said she needed to speak to Jack. Lily wasn't her normal self at all. She seemed very scared of something, but Joan couldn't imagine what it could possibly be. She just wished Lily would confide in her, talking might help. It was unlike Lily to be so secretive. The only other time she had been unwilling to say anything was on the subject of her past. Lily was being very mysterious that was for sure.

# Chapter Twelve

Lily turned up at work, not looking her best which earned her some very strange looks. She had shadows under her eyes which told of sleepless nights. She wore a deep frown which nothing could shift, it spoke of the perpetual worry she felt. She tried to stay focused on the job but it took a lot of effort. Usually she enjoyed her job but today she couldn't keep her mind on it, very scared and worried about what was soon to happen.

"What's going on down there?" asked one of the nurses, looking out of the window.

Lily went over and looked apprehensively out of the window, following the nurse's gaze. What they were seeing was a couple of official cars drawing up at the hospital entrance. Lily's heart leapt into her mouth, knowing exactly what was happening. Fear took over her body. Her face paled and nausea arose in her throat. Her breathing became shallow and she struggled to keep any of this from showing. She needed to keep everything as normal as possible but couldn't keep it together. She rushed from the ward needing to find the toilets. She put her head over the toilet and retched, nothing coming up though.

"Excuse me, is everything ok in there?" asked a voice.

"Yes, I'm all right," replied Lily, feeling far from all right, but not able to say that without an explanation.

It was obviously all happening as she had been told it would and she was scared.

Lily emerged from the toilet and rinsed her face under the tap. She looked out of the window and saw a crowd gathering outside. A man dressed in a black suit looked very sombre as he tried to disperse the crowd. The last thing anyone wanted was a crowd gathering to witness the arrest of the traitors. They didn't know how it would turn out, they were quite prepared for violence although they didn't want that to happen. They had no idea if the men were armed or not.

Lily went downstairs wanting to be there when the men were brought out. Only then would she start feeling safe again, knowing it was all over.

She hung back, not wanting to show herself, feeling safer that way, but needing to be there anyway. She didn't have long to wait as Colin and Eric were escorted out of the building. Colin appeared to be cooperative and looked at the ground as he was brought out. Eric on the other hand struggled and shouted, but no one could understand what he was saying as he shouted in German. There were gasps from those around as they realised what was happening. They didn't understand the words but it was obvious to all that here was a traitor.

"Speak English please," said one of his captors sternly.

"You will not win. You may have me but there are more of us and we will triumph," said Eric with a sneer. He no longer had to pretend to be English so he spoke with a strong accent and showed his feelings clearly. "Mein Fuhrer is the greatest and he will reign supreme throughout the world. Heil Hitler," he shouted, refusing to hide how he felt any longer. After all there was no need.

Colin, with a nod at the men holding him moved towards Eric and spoke, "Ernst we've been watching you for a long time. You may as well tell us who you reported to as we have so much information on your network anyway."

Ernst, for that was Eric's real name turned to Colin and spat into his face. "I was right not to trust you, you are one of them, a traitor to the Third Reich. You will not get away with this, that I can promise. I may not be able to do anything but there are others ready to avenge my capture. You better watch your back."

"You know now, so I have nothing to hide. I'm not a porter I was placed here by my superiors to keep an eye on you and find out who you worked for."

Lily gasped, unable to hide her shock. So that was why Colin had warned her off, he knew she would be in danger and wanted to keep her safe. She never had been in the danger she thought she was as only Colin knew what she had overheard. Yes, he was a spy but for the allies. She felt relief flood over her. Why had they not told her that? If she had known she might have felt more secure knowing the real spy didn't know anything about her. She supposed they couldn't tell her because they didn't want anything to be exposed for Colin's sake. It was on a need to know basis only. It would have put Colin in danger and nothing could be revealed because of national security. In the same way she wasn't allowed to say anything, they couldn't tell her anything either. Finally she was safe and it was all over, no more half heard conversations. She wobbled, close to collapse now it was over. She had kept going and tried to behave as normally as possible but now it had come to an end.

"Hey, are you all right?" asked a nurse she didn't recognise, concerned at how pale Lily was and how wobbly she looked.

"Yes, I'll be fine," replied Lily, knowing that this time she really would be ok. She sat down on a step before she fainted. She knew it was just a reaction to the strain she had been under that had now gone. It was the relief that seemed almost too much for her. An anti climax she thought.

Everyone dispersed as Ernst Muller was taken away. There was nothing else to see. He still insisted on speaking German, no one understood but realised it wasn't pleasant. He was a spy and would receive the ultimate punishment.

Colin approached Lily before he too disappeared, back to his life and work in the government. "Sorry you got caught up in that, and I'm sorry I couldn't tell you what was really going on. What you perceived as a threat was just a way of keeping you safe. It is unfortunate you overheard Ernst giving the Nazi greeting, as I needed more time to try and find out who was above him, who he reported to, but we couldn't keep going once you had reported what you knew. It was the right thing to do as it could have put you in danger."

Lily gave a weak smile. "Thanks," she said. "I was imagining all sorts after I heard that. I couldn't sleep last night absolutely convinced you would be coming after me now I knew too much."

"I'm very sorry about that, but you wouldn't have been in any danger as you were being closely watched. If there was any threat towards you action would have been taken sooner. Anyway I must go, I need to be there to interview the lovely Ernst Muller, although I doubt we will get anything out of him. I must say goodbye now. You won't be seeing me again."

Lily didn't respond, being in a daze. Her brain was still trying to process what had happened and realising she really was safe. It was all over.

Matron approached her and took her arm, "Come on let's get you inside for a nice cup of tea, that will revive you."

Lily stood up shakily, her legs not wanting to support her. If Matron hadn't been there she would have fallen. Leaning heavily on Matron she allowed herself to be taken inside.

Matron kept a close eye on Lily as she drank the tea. The colour came back in Lily's face which Matron was pleased to see, but she wasn't going to let Lily go until she could be sure she would be ok. Lily needed to be around someone at the moment to keep an eye on her.

Lily gave a weak smile, "Thanks I needed that."

"You must rest here for a while then when you have fully recovered you can go home and take the next couple of days off. It's been quite a strain on you the last few days and it's going to take time to get back to normal again. I'd like to bet you haven't been sleeping either." Matron lifted her eyebrows in query.

"You're right, I haven't slept, last night I went to bed and kept the poker next to me terrified someone was going to come for me."

Matron shook her head, "That's not good, you need sleep."

"I'm looking forward to going to bed, I'm so tired. I just hope I will be able to sleep without replaying it all in my head."

"We can make sure you sleep. A doctor can give you something that you can take as soon as you get home to guarantee sleep."

Suddenly Lily felt tears welling up inside and she was sobbing. The reaction was taking hold and she was able to cry out all the strain she had been under now it was all over and she no longer had to keep everything to herself. Matron reacted and held Lily until she quietened down. It was a violent outburst and didn't stop quickly. Matron didn't say anything just held her until the tears subsided. The tears stopped, leaving her eyes blood red and swollen from the outburst. She sniffed trying to clear her nose which was totally blocked from all the tears.

Matron was pleased the tears were stopping as she had started to become concerned the crying was turning to hysteria due to the severe reaction. She was unsure it was a good idea for Lily to be on her own at the moment and wondered if she needed a bed in the hospital where people were around if required and they could keep a close eye on her. She said this to Lily to see what Lily thought.

"No I'd rather go home, I have to be on my own sometime and anyway I have my neighbour, she could stay with me if necessary," said Lily, grateful for the thought.

"Good. As long as you won't be alone. I'll get those tablets for you that you must take as soon as you get home."

"I need to get a message to Jack and let him know everything is fine now and that I am all right."

"Of course. You can use this phone. I'll leave so you can have some privacy."

Lily shook her head, "Please stay, I don't want to be alone at the moment. Anyway I doubt I will be able to speak to him I'll just have to leave a message."

As expected Lily had to leave a message, but she was able to speak to the Squadron Leader which was a relief. At least it was someone who knew the situation and could relay the correct information to Jack so that he would understand it.

Lily stood up to leave, just wanting to go home to her bed, but first she would drop in on Joan. It would be a relief to be able to tell her the whole story.


………


Joan opened the door and seeing Lily breathed a sigh of relief and ushered her in. She had been worrying about Lily all afternoon. She noticed a difference immediately. Lily had a small smile on her face, was less pale and seemed more relaxed.

"You look better than when I last saw you," commented Joan.

"I feel it," said Lily taking a seat. "Put the kettle on and I'll tell you what's happened. I'm at liberty to tell you now it's all over."

Joan hastened to make the tea, wanting to hear what had been going on that had Lily so stressed and unlike herself.  She brought the teapot full of tea through then went back for the cups and saucers. She left the tea for some time waiting for it to become more like tea than hot water. There was no sugar to go in it but Lily wouldn't mind that, she knew the scarcity of food in these difficult times.

Joan leaned forward to see if the tea was ready to drink and poured it out. Lily had offered but Joan was still concerned that Lily might be a bit shaky still and spill it.  While they were sipping the hot liquid Lily began her story. Joan said nothing, letting Lily talk herself out. She gasped in horror as Lily told how she had heard the Nazi greeting.

"No wonder you were so scared and having nightmares about them," said Joan when Lily had finished her story. "I can't imagine what it must have been like for you the last few days, but I'm so pleased it's over for your sake as well as the country's sake. I can't believe there was a spy story going on all this time and you were involved. It's the sort of thing you see at the pictures not in reality."

"But at the pictures it seems exciting and action packed, the reality is much different. It was so very frightening. There was nothing exciting about it. I really did live in fear of my life. I didn't know who to trust and when I was told not to tell anyone it just made me more fearful. I wanted to tell you but apart from being told not to tell anyone I thought I might be putting you in danger as well."

"It's fine, I understand. You did the right thing. I would have been the same in your shoes."

"Of course I knew you weren't a spy and wouldn't pass on what I knew," said Lily, still trying to justify herself for not having spoken sooner.

Joan gave a laugh at the thought of being thought of as a spy. Lily seeing her burst out laughing. They both roared with laughter although not really knowing why. Lily found great relief from the laughter until Joan slapped her face.

"Sorry about that," she said, "You were sounded as if you were becoming hysterical."

"You did the right thing," said Lily. "Once I started I just couldn't stop, it was a release to let it out, even if it was in laughter. It was probably an inappropriate reaction but I just couldn't help it."

"It's ok, it's fine. I understand." Joan was only to pleased to see Lily looking herself once more.

"I'm glad it's over though. I would have gone bonkers if it had gone on much longer, then you would have been visiting me as well as Arthur."

"Don't say that," said Joan. "It's bad enough seeing Arthur in that place without you as well."

Lily changed the subject after that and they continued chatting for a while on mundane subjects before Lily left to go to bed, needing an early night.

## Chapter Thirteen

Lily was putting the last of the decorations up. She wanted it look as much like Christmas as possible. Jack was finally being given some time off and they had two whole days to spend together. She just wished Bobby could be with them as well. That would have made Christmas complete. They had discussed it in their letters but decided it would be better if he were to stay with Megan and Hugh. Jack would be home the next evening and they would spend Christmas Day and Boxing Day together before he had to be back. They would be going to Ted and Winnie's on Boxing Day where they would spend the day. They had been invited for Christmas Day as well but chose to be on their own. It had been some time since they had been together and it hadn't been just the two of them since Bobby had been born and then the war had started and they had been separated for so long.

Lily looked at the decorations and felt satisfied. The old paper chains still looked good, going from one side of the room to the other. It looked pretty, she thought to herself. Blues and yellows and greens. The room had a lovely festive look to it and the colours really lit the room up with the brightness. They crossed over in the middle with some beautiful red and orange. It created a warm feeling in the room, she decided. Just what they needed on a freezing winters day. She had a good feeling about this festive season. Together with Jack, just the two of them and then to that lovely couple who had become like parents to her. Jack had never met them and was looking forward to it very much. She knew he would love them as much as she did. He wouldn't be able to help himself she knew.


..........


"Oh darling, you don't know how much I've been looking forward to seeing you," said Jack, holding his wife tight, not wanting to let go.

"Help! You are squashing me," said Lily, laughing, for she felt the same.

"Sorry," said Jack, also giving a laugh, releasing her and looking at her, wanting to soak up everything about her in his heart and memories. He couldn't believe they were together even if it was only for two days. They would have to make every second count. He also couldn't wait to meet Ted and Winnie. They had captured Lily completely and they were so good for her, she was much more ready with a laugh and a joke now. Her eyes had lost that sad, serious look about her. Her past it seemed was truly that, in the past, of which he was pleased. She was becoming a completely different person. He loved who she had been and loved even more the person she now was.

He looked around the room, impressed with the decorations. "You've done well with the decorations, darling," he said. There was a warm glow about the room. He just wished Bobby could have been here as well but they had made the decision to leave him where he was settled as it was just a couple of days. Bobby would have loved this he thought. Oh well, they would have all the time in the world when this war ended.

"Do you want a cup of tea?" asked Lily. "It's all made."

"Definitely thanks, when have you ever known me pass on a cuppa."

Lily brought it through and poured the tea out for them both. "Sorry there are no mince pies and Christmas cake, but it was so difficult to get the ingredients in the shop."

"Never mind, I didn't expect anything. It's the same for everyone. We can still have a great time without that."

They sat sipping the hot liquid, enjoying being in each others presence. There was no need for words.

"How's Joan holding up?" asked Jack eventually, when they had finished their tea.

Lily looked sombre, "She's fine. Tries to hold it together but struggles. If you look underneath you see the pain she feels inside."

"It must be especially difficult this time of the year."

"I'm not sure it's any different to any other day really. Arthur is deteriorating. He is being kept sedated now as it's safer for him and the other patients and staff."

It's so sad, I can't even imagine what it must be like for her," said Jack.

They sat silently for a while thinking of Joan and Arthur.

"I did invite Joan to come to us for Christmas dinner but she said no. I think she wanted to give us time to ourselves."

"I'll go round there and invite her myself, she shouldn't be by herself at Christmas." Jack stood up, ready to go and speak to Joan.

Joan answered the door, surprised to see Jack stood there. He looked so handsome in his uniform, she thought, for a moment feeling a stab of jealousy towards her neighbours. They had each other and she had no one. She shook herself, why shouldn't they have some happiness together, after all Lily deserved it after the awful time she had growing up. She had no right to be envious really but she couldn't help how she felt.

"Hello Jack, great to see you back, come in." She stood aside to let her neighbour in.

"How are you doing?" he asked when inside and the door shut to keep the cold out.

"I'm fine," she said, but she looked anything other than fine thought Jack.

"I came round to see if you wanted to join us tomorrow. We don't like to see you on your own at Christmas and there will be no buses running so you won't see Arthur."

"No, it's fine. Thank you for asking though. I appreciate the thought but I won't be good company and it's not often you get to spend time together, so make the most of it."

"Don't worry about us, we would very much like it if you would spend some time with us tomorrow. I'm not taking no for an answer. You are coming and that's final. It's Christmas, and I don't want you moping about on your own," said Jack firmly.

Joan gave a small nod in agreement. Inside she was pleased as she had been dreading being by herself for Christmas.

"Thank you," she said, "It would be an honour, but I won't stay long as you should enjoy some time alone."

"You can stay as long as you like, we don't mind."

Jack went back home, lighter in his mind now that Joan had agreed to come.

Jack grinned at Lily as he stepped inside, rubbing his freezing hands together to try and warm them up a bit. "She agreed," he said triumphantly.

"I'm not even going to ask how you managed that," said Lily. "I tried and tried but couldn't get through to her."

"I gave her no option, said I wouldn't take no for an answer."

"You are a genius," said Lily melting into Jack's embrace. It was so nice to be together again, she thought.

"I know," said Jack with no ounce of modesty.

"You'll be getting too big for your boots soon," she said smiling and then they both started laughing.

How nice that Lily was so ready to laugh now, thought Jack. He couldn't wait to meet this couple who had worked such a miracle in his wife.

………

"Happy Christmas," said Lily the next morning when they woke up. She cuddled up happily to her husband. It was going to be a great day she just knew it.

They lay intertwined both comfortable and not really wanting to get up.

"I suppose we should get up, we don't know what time Joan will be here,"

"Hmm," murmured Jack, feeling lazy and enjoyed laying there cuddled up with his wife. "I just wish this war would end so we can be together all the time," he said.

"Come on," said Lily again, poking Jack in the ribs.

"Ow! What was that for?"

"I'm trying to encourage us both to get up. We don't want to waste the day in bed."

"I wouldn't mind that," said Jack with a mischievous grin on his face.

"Oh you wouldn't would you," said Lily with a hint of teasing in her voice. "Well I'm getting up. I don't want Joan turning up and finding us in bed, plus I have to get the dinner cooked. It's just a shame we haven't got cake or mince pies and the dinner will be more veggies than anything."

"Never mind, we will still enjoy the day. Everyone is in the same boat so it's not a problem," said Jack, reassuringly.

……..

When Joan turned up the dinner was ready so the three of them sat down to enjoy their meal. Lily had made it look appetising in spite of the scarce meat. The carrots and cabbage were chopped and set out attractively on the plates. The roast potatoes were just right, a golden brown and just the right crispness to them. As they ate the chatter was cheerful with plenty of laughter. Lily deliberately avoided the talk turning to Arthur.

She wanted this to be an enjoyable day for Joan, with nothing marring that for her friend. At first Joan was a bit quiet but soon joined in the chatter, making jokes and laughing along with Lily and Jack.

Jack looked around the table, satisfied. His wife was enjoying herself a long with their close friend. This year was the best Christmas, having Bobby would have made it complete but he was grateful for the time together anyway. Lily was so different from the serious, sad person she had always been. She had come out of her shell and opened right up. Her eyes were alight with laughter, and tomorrow he would be meeting the couple responsible for this change and he couldn't wait, he had a lot to thank them for. They had worked a miracle in his wife.

Dinner over, they sat back satisfied. Lily put the wireless on ready for the Kings speech. They never missed that, it was part of the ritual for Christmas Day. That over they sang some carols and other songs. In between they continued laughing and enjoying themselves with their chatter. They chatted and joked as if everything was normal, ignoring the fact that Jack was only around for a few days and would then be going back to base. Bobby was missing from the group which made Lily a bit sad but she refused to dwell on it. Of course Arthur was also not present but again they refused to dwell on the loved ones who couldn't be there on this special day.

The day passed quickly and soon it was time for Joan to leave. She had thoroughly enjoyed herself and was reluctant to withdraw from the party. It had been a pleasant day and she didn't want it to end.

"Thank you for having me, I really enjoyed myself," said Joan, reluctantly standing up. "I'm sorry I stayed so long, I hadn't  intended to. I wanted to leave you two to have the day to yourselves since you don't get the opportunity to be together very often.

"Don't worry about it," said Jack. "We enjoyed your company and are grateful you agreed to come. It's been a fun day."

Lily nodded in agreement, saying, "You made it a good day, a very special one. I bet old Hitler wouldn't like it if he knew we have been laughing and joking all day. He hasn't broken our spirit that is for certain. We will triumph over the evil of Nazism."

Joan took her leave after a hug from Jack and Lily. Jack and Lily collapsed into their chairs after Joan left and were silent in their own thoughts.

Lily was the first to break the silence, saying, "I'm really tired, I don't know about you, but I'm off to bed. Tomorrow will be another enjoyable day. I know you'll love Ted and Winnie."

"I am sure I will," said Jack with certainty. "I'm really looking forward to it."

Jack followed Lily upstairs as they rapidly got into bed. They lay quietly in each others arms, content with the silence and each other.

………

Winnie opened the door for Lily and Jack with a huge welcoming smile on her face. "Come in, come in," she said, ushering them in quickly for it was freezing outside. There wasn't any snow but there were icy patches.

As soon as they got inside Winnie hugged them both in turn. Jack was treated to a Winnie special, which was a huge hug that made him feel as if the breath was being squeezed out of him.

"I'm so pleased to meet you son," she said when she finally released him.

"Likewise," he said. "I've been looking forward to meeting you both for so long. I've heard so much about you and of course I've received all your letters."

Ted held out his hand to shake Jack's and then changed his mind and treated him to another huge hug. Jack was surprised by the strength of the hug from this slender man. He didn't look capable of it. Jack didn't know why he felt this way for Ted was anything but frail.

They all sat down and the chatter soon started. Winnie was quizzing Jack to get to know him better. Although she had known for a long time that he was right for her girl, for that is how she felt about Lily. She was so grateful for the day that Ted had spoken to her about Lily, even if she had given her own brand of punishment. She gave a broad smile.

"What are you grinning like a Cheshire cat about?" asked Ted, knowing Winnie too well.

Winnie told them all what she had been thinking.

"Yes, I remember that vividly," said Ted. "You hit me over the head with your secret weapon. You should go over to Germany and hit Hitler over the head, he'd be so stunned at your audacity that he would end the war with immediate effect."

They all broke into laughter, including Jack who was quickly realising why Lily had responded to their love and humour.

"You think so do you?" asked Winnie when the laughter stopped. "Are you saying you want me killed are you," she said with a threatening note in her voice.

Ted, realising where this was going, winked at Lily who grinned, for she knew what would happen next. Jack just looked bemused by it, not quite sure what was going on now.

"Of course I don't my darling, but you have to admit when you get going everyone is stunned into silence."

"Is that so?" asked Winnie, still in that dangerous voice, that spelled trouble for her longsuffering husband.

"I think you should try it and see, just think you would be hailed a hero."

"What if I don't want to be a hero?"

"But don't you want the opportunity to end the war now rather than later."

Winnie stood up, cradling her handbag tightly to her. She went across to Ted and raising it above her head brought it down on to him.

Laughter broke out once more. Even Jack laughed until his sides ached. He hadn't laughed this much for a very long time, if ever. He could see now why Lily loved them so much, they were a real hoot. He looked across at his wife, wiping her eyes, for she was crying with laughter. Her whole face was alight including her eyes. He knew she would never have that sad, serious look again and was so very grateful for this hilarious couple who had done so much for his beloved wife. As he looked around the room he felt enveloped by the warmth of this couple that just emanated from them. It was obvious they didn't have much in material terms but they certainly made up for that in their huge personalities. No one would ever feel left out with these two around. They wouldn't allow it. He had been made to feel at ease the minute he walked through the door, and knew instantly that he was accepted by them.

"Earth to Jack," said Winnie, bringing Jack back to the present from his reverie.

"Sorry I was miles away," said Jack blushing at the accusatory look in Winnie's eye and something else which he couldn't identify.

Ted and Lily exchanged a look and a secret grin, they knew exactly where this was going.

"Oh, you don't want to be here don't you?" queried Winnie still in that same tone, that boded ill although Jack was still too inexperienced to notice.

"Of course I want to be here, I've been looking forward to it ever since I knew I was going to get leave. I'm sorry if I have offended you. It wasn't intentional."

Winnie stood up and before he knew what was happening he felt the full force of the handbag on his head.

"Ow," he said involuntarily.

Ted and Lily just cracked up, doubling up with laughter at what had just happened. Jack's face was a picture, a mixture of bemusement and something else although they couldn't describe it.

Jack looked around the room seeing everyone else laughing as they had never laughed before and he too started laughing as well. He had well and truly walked into that, but he was still a novice when it came to Winnie. He was certain he would face more of that before the end of the day.

Jack looked across at his wife, her eyes alight with laughter. He was satisfied. He knew if anything happened to him she would be okay. Gone was the serious, sad face that had haunted her and now the smile and laughter lit her face right up to her eyes. This was all down to Ted and Winnie, they had been good for her, she was in very good hands with them he recognised. He joined in the hilarity with them and the laughter filled the room like music.